SURESH KOHLI (b. 1947) is a multi-dimensional personality: poet, literary critic, editor, translator, film historian and documentary filmmaker. He has over 30 published works (including a novel) and a hundred literary and cultural short films to his credit. His films have been screened in Australia, France, Germany, Spain, Nepal and the UK, apart from in India. He lives and works in New Delhi.

SARDARJI
AND OTHER STORIES

KHWAJA AHMAD ABBAS

Edited by
Suresh Kohli

OM
Om Books International

Published in 2014 by

OM

Om Books International

Corporate & Editorial Office
A-12, Sector 64, Noida 201 301
Uttar Pradesh, India
Phone: +91 120 477 4100
Email: editorial@ombooks.com
Website: www.ombooksinternational.com

Sales Office
4379/4B, Prakash House, Ansari Road
Darya Ganj, New Delhi 110 002, India
Phone: +91 11 2326 3363, 2326 5303
Fax: +91 11 2327 8091
Email: sales@ombooks.com
Website: www.ombooks.com

ISBN: 978-93-83202-17-1

10 9 8 7 6 5 4 3 2 1

Printed in India

CONTENTS

Introduction 7

1. All That Two Hands Can Carry! 19
2. 1,000 Nights on a Bed of Stones 31
3. Death of an Emperor 51
4. The Gun 61
5. The Lamp That Burns All Night 73
6. The Naked Fakir 82
7. Fathers and Sons 92
8. The Five Faces of Mother India 114
9. Rice 144
10. Ajanta 155
11. Cold Wave 190
12. Sardarji 206
13. Letar from a Child to Mahatma Gandhi 221
14. Twelve Hours 229

The Last Interview 243

INTRODUCTION

A masterful practitioner of prose, Khwaja Ahmad Abbas (1914-1987) has for long been diminished as a creative writer, both in Urdu and in English: the two main languages he used for creative communication. One of the reasons could be the multi-dimensional aspect of his personality, which did not define him solely as a writer of fiction. He deliberately shunned all labels and dogmas and preferred to call himself a "communicator". He was a journalist in Urdu and English simultaneously. He was a playwright, novelist and short story writer in the two languages he was at ease with, even though some of his writings, paradoxically, first appeared in Hindi—a language he understood but could never read or write in directly. He was a successful scriptwriter but a flop director despite having made some outstanding films.

I interviewed him in 1982 to discuss this and he said, "Just because I write in two languages principally and a third language occasionally, nobody is prepared to take me seriously. That is, nobody belonging to the vested interests of the establishment of these three languages. Otherwise, so far as readers are concerned, the letters I get in these languages make a staggering total. They keep me and my secretary extremely busy deciphering them and replying to the questions asked and demands made by correspondents. Actually, since my writings are translated into almost all the languages of India, at least a quarter of the letters are in languages other than English, Urdu or Hindi, for instance, Malayalam, in which, for some reason, I seem to be popular, or Tamil where about a dozen of my works have been translated in the last two or three years. This makes me both proud and humble."

And that has, indeed, been the tragedy encompassing all of Abbas's creative endeavours: his range became his enemy. His capacity for communication cast a sort of "halo" around him that rubbed the sheen off his long and short fiction, which, on reissue, is finally beginning to draw the attention it deserves in both Urdu and English. Though many writers in the recent past have sought to depict both, the seamy and reputable sides of Hindi cinema, Abbas was the first to write a full-fledged novel—*Boy Meets Girl*—that exposed the sham behind the glam. Sadly, critics and academics in India have, except in the early phase of Indian writing in English, failed to take cognisance of this pioneering work. Even his monumental novel, *Inqilab*—chronicling the Indian freedom struggle, beginning with the Jallianwala Bagh massacre and ending with the Gandhi-Irwin Pact, first published in English in 1955—was largely ignored. The sequel to *Inqilab, The World is My Village,* which begins with the Munich crisis of 1938 and concludes with the Independence of India and Partition, appeared in 1983. At the time of his death in 1987, Abbas had been working on a third book but sadly, the incomplete manuscript got destroyed in the tragic events that followed his untimely passing away: a relative gave away his apartment and along with it, his possessions including books, memorabilia, manuscripts and documents. This collection included the incomplete script that was to form part of the third book.

In the brief preface to his autobiography, *No Man is an Island*, he had written: "It has taken years of working on literary potboilers and filmic 'blood boilers', from *Dharti Ke Laal* to *The Naxalites*, to find time to complete the second volume which can be read (and even enjoyed) as a separate literary entity. The third part will be hopefully written quicker—provided I manage to keep myself alive for another few years."

Elaborating further, he sought to answer the question: 'Is it an autobiographical novel?' This was asked when the first volume, *Inqilab*, was published, and it will be asked again. The answer is that a novelist's life and experiences do get into his creative writings. Tolstoy, Chekhov, Dickens and Sarat Chandra Chatterjee did not write autobiographical novels, yet their lives were reflected and sometimes reported in their writings. To that extent, *Inqilab* and *The World is My Village* may also be said to be partly autobiographical." Incidentally, the Urdu edition of the novel got published decades later, in 1976, for which the author won an award of ₹3,000 from Urdu Academy, Lucknow.

"*Inqilab* has been my most satisfying creative work," he told me in the course of another interview. "It took me nine years to write. I was a Sunday writer, in the sense that I could work on the novel only on Sundays because on the other days I worked in a newspaper to earn my livelihood. Eventually, I had to take a month's leave to finish it. That is why, I think, good and great novels are not being written in India: perhaps there is a lack of response. Trivial stories and novels are being written. But it is because the writers do not have the stamina. The publisher's advances are not adequate enough to meet the needs of the writer."

During his lifetime, Abbas did not hold a grudge about the fact that the literati had "sometimes sneeringly labelled my novels and short stories as 'mere journalese'. The fact that most of them are inspired by aspects of contemporary historical reality—as sometimes chronicled in the press—it is sufficient to put them beyond the pale of literary creation. I have no quarrel with the critics. Maybe I am an unredeemed journalist and reporter, masquerading as a writer of fiction. But I have always believed that while the inner life of Man undoubtedly is, and should be, the primary concern of literature, this inner personal life impinges upon the life of the community and of humanity at every critical turning point of human experience. John Donne said, 'No Man is an island…' and one may add that even if he is, no island is free from the inroads of the sea, as no man is free from the impact of social forces and the life around him."

When it comes to Abbas's short fiction, his name does not feature in the A-list of Urdu short story writers despite having a landmark story like "Sardarji" or "Ek Insaan Ki Maut" (or as Khushwant Singh preferred to name it, "The Death of Shaikh Burhanuddin", in his English translation). His very first story "Ababeel" or "Sparrows" is a moving story of remorse and disillusionment that instantly found a place in a West German anthology of the 100 best stories of the world, which also had two others by Rabindranath Tagore and Mulk Raj Anand. Talking about the origin of "Sparrows", Abbas said, "I wrote this story in 1937 when I was living in a chawl in Bhendi Bazaar in Bombay (many other stories here belong to the first few years of his landing up in Bombay and working as a reporter and sub-editor in the now defunct daily, *Bombay Chronicle*).

"I wrote it originally in Urdu and it was called 'Ababeel'. It was my first attempt at short-story writing in any language. The *ababeel* are a special kind of sparrow who build nests with clay and not straw. At that time, I didn't think about how the idea struck me. I thought it came out of my imagination. But 20 years later, when the late Krishan Chander interviewed me for an Urdu literary magazine, he asked me to recall the genesis of my first short story. I told him that the first time I saw a nest of the *ababeel* was when, as a child, I used to visit my maternal grandfather's house where he was living as a lonely widower (he was an intellectual and the son of the poet Hali). The *ababeel* were always creating a racket as their nest was in the roof above the easy chair where the bearded Baba (as we used to call Grandfather) used to relax. He was a man of quick temper—easy to rouse but quick to subdue his anger. He would beat a servant for insubordination in the morning and give him ₹5 as *bakhsheesh* in the afternoon.

"Once, in a flash of anger, he ordered the nest of the *ababeel* to be destroyed. But by the time the servant had climbed the ladder to do it, Baba's temper had cooled off. 'Let it be,' he said and, to his dying day, the *ababeel* were fluttering and hovering above him. Then, at the age of six or seven, I accompanied my family on a visit to a village near Panipat that belonged to one of my uncles. It gave me a shock to see in what utter poverty the peasants were living. Some of them would bring sacks of grain on donkeys to our house and unload them in our courtyard. They were so poor that the greatest luxury for them after delivering the grain would be to spend one pie at the shop of the ice-seller and get a glass of iced sherbet! The wheat-grain at that time was being sold at the rate of 25 seers (or 50 kg) for a rupee. But even then, I would often wonder why the peasant slaved year-round and then bring their sacks of grains to the house of the landlords. How long would it continue?

"The character of my grandfather and the atmosphere in the village that I had seen as a child mixed in the crucible of my imagination to create this story. Krishan Chander, when he heard of it, said, "The *chidiya* (sparrow) is caught at last!"

The title story in this selection, "Sardarji", was mercilessly attacked by both, the Muslims and the Sikhs, and led to the author being dragged to court; with the first of these instances taking place in Allahabad. Fearing for his life, Mrs. Sarojini Naidu, then Governor of what is now Uttar Pradesh, invited him to her house and requested him to read the story to her. After listening to it, she reportedly had tears in her eyes, wiping which, she told him, "This is a very touching story. But you are a fool. Is this the time to write such stories?" When I asked about this incident in another interview, he said,"No,

I didn't agree with her then and I don't agree with her now. That was her way of showing affection for the writer because at that time she was worried I might be murdered, though there was no such danger. You see, the Sikhs were blamed for saying that I should be murdered and some did say things in the Gurudwaras and so on. Their minds were inflamed by the first line in the story because I had begun by saying: "*Main sikhon se nafrat karta tha*" (I used to hate the Sikhs). Khushwant was clever enough to phrase this the way he does in his rendition, and rightly so, not only because he was playing safe but because good translation does require a rework, according to the idiom of the language of translation.

Abbas narrated an incident about the court case: "I had a very interesting experience in the court where an old Sardarji with a long beard came to give evidence. He had filed the case from Jhansi. He asked me: 'Why did you write such a story against us?' I said, 'Sardarji, your opinion about me is perhaps wrong. I wish that you hear the whole story from me, only if you can spare an hour and don't get angry with me until you have heard the entire story.' So, he came home and stayed with me for an hour. I read out the whole story to him. At the end, his eyes were filled with tears. He got up and embraced me, and said, 'The writer of such a story should be awarded a medal.' And he went to the court and said, 'I want to withdraw my charges and am going back to Jhansi. I think Abbas Sahib has written a very good story.'"

But that was not the end. Abbas went on to say, "There was another episode at the Kashmir border, where fighting was going on at that time. I had gone to the border with a party of correspondents and we were sent to different outposts. I went to one outpost alone and that was being manned only by three Sardars. They were sitting in the dugout with a candle stuck in a bottle. At that time, I used to carry the story with me in my pocket so that if there was any danger I could read out the story.

"The Sikh officer said, '*Aap ka naam kya hai*?' I told them that my name is Khwaja Ahmad Abbas. They whispered something to each other. One of them said, 'Do you write stories?' I said, 'Yes, I do write stories and I've written "Sardarji" if you're referring to that story. They said, 'Why did you write that against us?' I said, 'Would you like to hear the story? I shall narrate it to you right now.' They said, 'We'll hear it.' I said, You won't kill me, will you, until you have heard the end of the story?' They laughed, and said: 'No, no, we won't kill you.' So I narrated the story and they too, like the Sardarji in the court, were overwhelmed by the story. They shook my hand and said that I would have to drink rum with them, which I had previously refused because I am a teetotaller." All this had happened in 1948, although matters seem no better even now, as objections against some writers and artists, demanding they be dragged to the courts for their written work, continue to make news.

Abbas had simply recounted an experience he had witnessed. In his own words: "Actually, this is a true story because a Sardarji did save the life of my nieces and a cousin, but his death did not take place. That's the only fictitious part of the story. The property of my relatives had been looted by an RSS gang that had been ravaging the whole city at the time. The Sardarji told his children to go and participate in the looting and bring back whatever they could. And it is only due to that that some of the property was saved. Whatever was brought to the Sardarji's house was given to my relatives, who were hidden inside the kitchen. The Sardarji took out his *kirpan* and said, *'Jab tak hum zinda hain, tumko koi haath nahin laga sakta'* (No one can touch you as long as we are alive). So that gave me the inspiration to write that end—the fact that he could have been killed."

I must speak about Khushwant, whose translation of "Sardarji" is in this book. He had been challenging death for the past few years, even naming one of his last compilations *Death at My Doorstep*, but finally it called on the morning of March 20, 2014. The country's best known *Sardar* missed the century mark and bid a silent adieu at the ripe age of 99.

Now that he is gone, do I have an answer to the question he had asked me at the time I was making a film on him: "Why do people live so long if they can't maintain their health and sanity?" He had obviously been referring to celebrities like Mulk Raj Anand, Raja Rao, RK Narayan, Sanyal and others.

I did not meet him during the last two years of his life, for whenever I called, his answer, in Punjabi, would be, "I am totally deaf." I, however, did call his bluff by landing up at his apartment at his drinking time. As had been his wont after his wife, Kanwal's, death, he was surrounded by a bevy of women of all shades, colours, ages and dimensions. But, sharp-witted that he was, he obviously tried to cover up, and welcomed me anyway, deputing me to be the bartender. Though I have come across countless Sikhs, he, indeed, will remain the most notable one.

Coming back to Abbas, his motto in life had been "to mirror life realistically but also critically so that things can improve. The improvement of Man, I think, is the greatest mission of a writer, intellectual or creative artist. If he disregards this mission, he cannot be a good writer," he told me in the course of an interview I conducted with him in Bombay for *India Today* in May 1976, on the eve of his departure for the US for medical treatment.

Through his writing, Abbas also tried to dissolve the boundaries present in writing various forms. During one of many elaborate sessions of candid confessions, he told me, "I have personally tried to eliminate the difference between a short story and a novel by writing long short stories or shorter novels. For instance, the short novel, *The Walls of Glass*, is, I think, quite well constructed. I will share a secret with you. This was first written many, many years ago in Urdu and it somehow got lost in a heap of papers when I shifted my office from an apartment to my garage. When I rediscovered it, I took it along with me to Canada when I went there for treatment and reworked it afresh in English. Frankly, I do not follow any set pattern or plan to narrate something with the language in mind. That comes in automatically. For instance, the story 'Ajanta' got written during a single sitting in Aurangabad during the journey back to Bombay, and it was completed by the time the train arrived at Bombay Central."

Another story in this collection, "The Gun", presumably written in the early 1980s, is dedicated to the late actor Smita Patil, who had worked in his film, *The Naxalites*, and who he had wanted to repeat in one of his other projects. "The Naked Fakir" was for his great grandnephew, the incomparable Pankaj Kapoor, who not only acted in a short film with the same name but even in Abbas's signing-off venture, *Ek Aadmi,* the print or the negative of which remains untraceable despite it being financed by the National Film Development Council.

In an introductory letter to one of Abbas's earlier short story collections, the late doyen of Indian fiction in English, Mulk Raj Anand, wrote: "The strength of your short stories, my dear Abbas, lies in the fact that you have grasped the weaknesses of your characters amid their strengths."

All the stories here have been selected to provide a glimpse into the mind and work of the forgotten legend, Abbas, born exactly a century ago into one of the 40,000 Muslim families in Panipat which refused to migrate to Pakistan during Partition. It is difficult to pigeonhole him into a specific box because he refused to stick to a single arena in order to put across his ideas, feelings, emotions and reflections. He wished to communicate to a larger audience and that is why he chose every possible avenue available to him.

Suresh Kohli
New Delhi

ALL THAT TWO HANDS CAN CARRY!

The distant barking of the dogs woke up Sakharam. In the dark, it sounded peculiar, even eerie. It was more like wailing. There was also a strange fluttering of a thousand unseen wings, as if the birds, too, were alarmed.

He looked at his wrist watch; its luminous hands showed the time to be five minutes to four. The watchman in the bazaar, he knew, would go off-duty at four thirty. That would give him roughly an hour to ransack the shop!

Theft, house-breaking, tinkering with locks and safes, none of these activities was new to him. During the last three years he had been to jail several times—he did not even remember exactly how many times. Twice, within the last two years, he had been externed from Bombay. This time they had told him plainly that if they saw him within city limits, they would straightway chargesheet him, even if he had not committed a crime.

So Sakharam had come to Poona. But the climate was not conducive to petty crime. On cold nights, people slept with their doors and windows closed. The policemen were constantly on the prowl. Under the circumstances, what could a poor fellow—or a poor thief—do? In a couple of days, he ran out of the little money he had with him. He had even thought of returning home to his village; after all, it was not more than a hundred miles from Poona. But with that face, would he be able to confront his wife? Hadn't he, on the eve of his departure from the village, sworn before his wife in the temple of Vithoba that he would come back only when he had enough money to redeem his land from the *sahukar,* to repair the walls and roof of his little hut, and to buy two Kolhapuri bullocks? How modest were his ambitions—two acres of land, a pair of oxen, a plough, four mud walls, and a thatched roof over them. And, of course, Savitri!

Whenever he thought of Savitri, Sakharam felt a pang in his heart. There wasn't a girl in the village who was half as beautiful as his wife. She was always smiling, even when there was not enough to eat in the house. If some girlfriend ostentatiously sympathised with her, she would say, "What do I care? Let God preserve the two hands of my man, and all will be well. You just wait and see." There was only one disappointment for Sakharam, so far as his wife was concerned. Though they had been married for five years, she had not presented him with a bonny boy—not even a girl child.

As he thought of her, Sakharam smiled in the dark. He spread out his rough and calloused hands in front of him. He could feel each hand by touching it with the other, but he could not see them. They had ploughed, and they had scattered the seed; they had transplanted the paddy seedlings, and they had wielded the sickle to reap the harvest.

After the harvest, he had filled the sacks of grain, loaded them in his bullock cart, and driven to the market to the *sahukar's* shop. And the man of money had consulted his big red ledgers and told Sakharam that the year's harvest was not sufficient to repay the debt. He had to sell his remaining bullock, the other having already died of old age and undernourishment. He had to drag back the cart, by yoking himself to it like an ox. That day, Sakharam decided to go to Bombay.

He had heard there was plenty of work to be found in the city—all that was needed was a stronger pair of hands. There was no demand for them in mills. So, with his hands, he had carried baskets of fruits and vegetables in the municipal market, unloaded sacks full of rice and wheat from the goods trains and loaded them into trucks, and from the trucks transferred them to the godowns. Then, after a tiring day, he would retire for the night on the footpath. The colourful neon lights of the cinemas winked invitingly, the half-naked Memsahibs on the film posters smiled tantalisingly, but Sakharam refused to be lured by the sirens of the cinema. After all, his own Savitri was more beautiful than any of them! She was beautiful and she was real. Why should he pay money to see merely ugly shadows of those *Memsahibs* on the screen?

And so, tied round his waist in the folds of the end of his *dhoti,* his savings grew from five to 10, from 10 to 20, 50, 100, 200 rupees. And all the time, he could imagine his land, his village, his bullocks, his Savitri, coming nearer to him.

One day, he got up from sleep later than usual, muttered the name of God as he yawned and stretched his limbs to remove the stiffness of sleeping on cold and hard stones, and, under his shirt, felt the folds of his *dhoti* where the packet of money was normally tied to his waist. It was all gone. He had been robbed of months of hard labour of his stinting and saving, he had been robbed of his dreams.

"Where is that rascal?" He shouted wildly.

"Which rascal?" someone asked him, "So many rascals sleep on this footpath."

"The one who was lying here beside me. How sweetly he was talking to me last night! I told him—yes, the fool that I am, it was I myself that told him—I had saved up ₹350, and he congratulated me and said he envied me. But where has the rascal gone?"

An old, crippled beggar, who sat in a corner and was the silent witness of everything that went on on the footpath, now spoke. "You won't see that rascal, Bhikoo. He must be drinking away your money in some liquor dealer's den."

It took him three days to secure the underworld of the city. He looked for Bhikoo in every illicit liquor bar and distillery. He met some strange characters in the bootleg business and they made him tempting offers. "Come into our trade, and you will make in a month all that you have lost." But Sakharam was obsessed with only one thought—he had to find Bhikoo, who had not only robbed him but made him look like a fool. He had to get even with him. At last, on the fourth day, he caught up with him in a liquor dealer's hut in the odorous slums of Dharavi. There was a bottle, a glass and a plate of roasted groundnuts on the table in front of him and he already looked drunk.

Sakharam caught him by the throat and shouted, "You rascal! Where is my money?"

Bhikoo didn't deny taking his money, he only said, "Don't be so excited, brother. You will have your money."

Sakharam loosened his hold. Bhikoo put his hands in his pocket and took out a handful of loose coins and flung them on the table. "There—take them. That's all I have." Sakharam pounced on the cash. "But you stole 350. This is not even ₹4. Where is the rest of my money?"

"Here," Bhikoo pointed to his tummy. Then he laughed aloud, "Drunk it all, it was wonderful. Thank you, brother, thank you."

Then Bhikoo turned to Sakharam, "Sit down, friend. I suggest you also drink. We can order two more bottles."

"I don't drink," replied Sakharam, but he sat down, still glaring at Bhikoo.

"That's the trouble. You don't drink and with so much money, you have to sleep on the footpath. Drink, my friend. It is your money that has paid for this liquor."

Saying this, he poured out a glass and held it up for Sakharam.

Sakharam thought, "Maybe he is right. After all he *has* bought it with my money." He took the glass and tentatively sniffed the liquor. The odour, like rotting garbage, repelled him. But with an effort he gulped it down. First it seemed a double-edged knife was going down his throat. But after a while, that feeling was replaced by a wave of soft warmth that was running through his veins.

Bhikoo, meanwhile, had re-filled his glass. "Have another, my brother."

Sakharam drained the second glass, too.

He had just put back the tumbler on the table and Bhikoo was raising the liquor bottle to pour out a third peg, when Sakharam noticed the golden watch on Bhikoo's wrist.

"This also you have brought with my money?" he shouted, suddenly angry.

Bhikoo took off the brand new wrist watch and handed it over to Sakharam. "Take it, my friend. Bought it only today from a smuggler who gave it to me at a concession price. Made in Switzerland. Shows the right time—even in the dark."

After two years, that watch on the wrist of Sakharam, with its luminous dial, was still showing the time in the dark. It was four minutes past four. Sakharam thought, "How slowly time passes." He couldn't begin his work till half past four. Looking at the watch, he thought gratefully of Bhikoo, who was again in jail but who, by stealing Sakharam's money, had shown him the way to a new and lucrative career.

He began with petty thefts, slowly graduating to more ambitious burglaries. But he still never had enough money to return to his village, to redeem his land, to acquire a couple of bullocks and to buy some saris and a few trinkets for Savitri. The traders who clandestinely bought stolen goods only paid a pittance. Moreover, whatever Sakharam "earned" was spent on eating and drinking and entertaining his new friends.

In Poona one evening, as it grew dark, he tried to run away after snatching a large purse from the hand of a middle-aged woman. But that one started screaming at such a loud pitch that people rushed to her from all directions. Sakharam hurriedly took out a few ₹10 notes, and threw away the tell-tale purse. Running at top speed towards the S.T. Bus Stand, he arrived there just as a bus was about to depart. He got into the bus as it started moving.

The conductor asked him, "Where do you want to go?" Sakharam, still panting for breath, replied, "Wherever this bus is going."

The bus conductor mentioned the name of some place which Sakharam could not hear properly because of the clatter of the bus changing gears and his own nervousness and excitement. Then, the conductor said "seven rupees", and Sakharam handed over one of the ₹10 notes he had stolen from the woman and pocketed the change of ₹3 which was returned to him.

Early in the morning, the bus reached the terminus and Sakharam, sleepy-eyed after the night-long journey, got down from the vehicle. He had imagined a village, but he saw that it was a bustling town with a bazaar and shops full of goods. Goods that were worth the attention of a professional thief!

Sakharam decided to spend a few days there for reconnaissance. He wandered through the bazaar, apparently aimlessly, but with a purposeful glint in his eyes. He mentally noted which shop sold what, but he was mainly interested in saris, cloth, radios, jewellery. He also kept his eyes open for iron safes, for that is where the cash must be. At night, the bazaar was patrolled by watchmen but Sakharam had noticed that they all retired at half-past four. That was the time for his operation to begin. Within an hour, he would be able to go through three or four shops, and by the time the bazaar opened, he would be far away on the way to his village.

On the outskirts of the town, there was a tin-roofed shack which was empty. There were several such houses which had been abandoned by the workers, who left on completion of the dam. At night, Sakharam quietly slipped in and slept there. There was nothing in the hut but four walls and a roof, but it protected him from the biting cold and the freezing wind. Far away, to one side, he could see the lights on the dam, while on the other side and much nearer were the glittering lights of the town. Lying in his dark hut, he often thought it was the only island of darkness in this ocean of lights. Was the darkness only in his hut or in his heart, too?

No, this was some other kind of darkness. Even the lights on the dam and the town were drowned in it. Far away, in the depths of darkness, indistinct specks of light glimmered—like stars reflected in a pool of dark and deep water. Not only did he feel suffocated in the dark, it seemed like his life itself was being choked. Or maybe it was only his mind playing tricks on him. He looked at the luminous dial of the watch. It was 20 minutes past four. Now he had better start. It would take him at least 10 minutes to reach the shops in the bazaar. He had hardly got up on his feet when he heard a peculiar rumbling sound as if a train was passing through a tunnel, or an aeroplane, flying low, was about to crash to the ground. But the sound came from deep down in the earth, and he could feel the ground slipping from under his feet. When his legs faltered, he tried to support himself against the wall. But the moment he touched it, he felt the wall, too, was rocking. If he had taken liquor that evening he would have ascribed these sensations to the influence of alcohol. But he hadn't touched a drop for three days. Then what possibly could it be...?

"Earthquake!" The thought flashed through his mind and in the next moment, the tottering walls and the clattering roof came down crashing on his head.

When he regained consciousness, the first thing he noticed was the pungent smell of sulphur and a suffocating cloud of dust. The darkness was so dense that you could cut it with a knife. Sakharam could feel a trickle slowly creeping down his forehead. When his hand touched it, he winced with pain and knew it was blood. There was a wound on his head from which blood was oozing. He had scratches and cuts on his legs, arms, and on one side of his face. But this was no time to worry about these minor injuries. The tingling pain had brought him out of consciousness and now his mind was preoccupied only with one exciting thought. If this hut had collapsed over him, the roofs and the walls of the shops in the bazaar, too, must have fallen. He wouldn't have to spend any time breaking open the locked doors. But was there still time? He looked at his watch. 4.30. The earthquake had struck only 10 minutes ago.

Removing the corrugated tin sheet that had fallen over him, he got up on his feet. On all sides were piles of fallen bricks. Groping his way in the dark, stumbling, limping, he started in the general direction of the town. The lights on the dam and the town had all been switched off. Now his work was made much easier.

The darkness was slowly turning into a dirty pallor of pre-dawn. In the dim light, he saw the dark outlines of the fallen houses. It seemed like the whole town had come down like a house of cards. Clouds of dust were rising from the debris. There were gaping cracks in the road. Men, women, and children were buried under piles of bricks and stones. Those who had not died instantaneously or been knocked unconscious were crying out for help or just whining incoherently. But Sakharam was preoccupied only with one thought—this God-sent opportunity to clean out the bazaar must not be missed. He had no time to save someone's life. Today, he would think only of himself.

In the bazaar, not a single shop was left intact. Their goods lay there in the open amidst the debris, under fallen bricks and tiles. Like a man possessed, he fell upon the scattered display of luxury articles. From the silk store, he snatched a dozen saris and a few rolls of cloth. From the next shop, he took two radios. Trinkets and jewellery lay in the dust—he picked up two handfuls without worrying to verify whether they were silver or gold. A safe had been flung out, face down. He tried to set it right but it was too heavy and with all the injuries he had received, he was not strong enough. The cash-box from another shop had come flying on to the road. He picked it up, tried to open it, and when he couldn't, he flung it in the heap which was already too big. So he used one of the saris to pile everything in and tie a bundle. It was quite heavy, too. His legs wobbled under its weight, but he managed to totter along. He was in a hurry to be away before anyone arrived there to question him.

Slowly, dawn was breaking. In the east, the forms of the clouds, the hills, and the dam were emerging from the grey nothingness. The ruins of the town were also taking distant shapes. Everywhere there was desolation and an eerie silence. It seemed that the town was dead, the world was dead, there was only one survivor, and he was running away with all the loot of the earth.

No, he thought, someone else is also alive! The sudden cry of a child unnerved him, as if it had come not from outside but from within his own heart. He turned to look and saw the ruins of a house and among them the dead bodies of a man and a woman. It took him some time to recognise the child: a boy of about a year who had miraculously survived, sitting naked among a pile of bricks and piteously crying.

Sakharam saw the child, and immediately turned away—as if the child had caught him stealing. He quickened his steps to get far beyond the reach of the child's voice. But the child started crying more lustily. Sakharam's steps slackened and then stopped. He could not go forward. He felt as if it was the son of whom they had always dreamt but who was not yet born out of the womb of Savitri.

He looked back at the child. Carrying the load on his head, he walked upto him. He wondered if it was possible to carry the bundle as well as pick up the baby boy. But he had only one pair of hands. They could either support the bundle of loot or carry the child in his arms.

He flung the bundle from his head and ran to the child with outstretched hands. The child came into his lap, then whimpered a little as if swallowing his last few sobs. Then he clung to Sakharam as if he had found his father again.

Sakharam cast but a fleeting look at the bundle in which were all the things had craved and desired—except one. This one he had in his arms. Then he hugged the precious living bundle to his chest and set out on his way.

From behind the dam, the sun was casting a baleful look at the destruction of Koyna. But a soft silken ray of sun fell on Sakharam as the child he carried in his arms smiled a toothless smile through the tears that still lurked in his eyes.

ONE THOUSAND NIGHTS ON A BED OF STONES

The first night is always the hardest. That is what the old beggar told me when I spread some newspapers and laid myself beside him on what the poet might describe as my "stony couch".

I had carefully selected a dark corner of the footpath in an obscure by-lane, for on that first night, I was terribly shy and self-conscious about my degradation.

It had been a month since I arrived in Bombay, but in 30 days I seemed to have aged many years, from the hopeful 20s to the frustrated 50s. From Hathras in Uttar Pradesh, I had travelled to Bombay in overcrowded Third Class, but not without a ticket. In my pocket I had more than ₹20, a school leaving certificate and my father's old watch, not to mention a heart full of youthful ambition and the determination to succeed.

I had a letter of introduction to the friend of a friend who worked in a textile mill, requesting him to accommodate me till I could find a job and a place of my own. He and his wife and two children lived in a chawl in Parel in a little fifth-floor room, which also served as a kitchen and bathroom. Behind the long row of rooms, there was a narrow verandah leading to the communal lavatory. There I lay at night, open to the smoke from the factory chimney and the poison-gas odours from the lavatory with its flush arrangement chronically out of order.

The whole day, I tramped from factory to workshop to office to studio to employment exchange, so that by the time I hit my bed, I was too tired to bother about latrine smells or the symphony of all the snorers who lay, like me, through the entire length of the verandah. It was uncomfortable to sleep there, but at least it was respectable, for I did have a roof over my head.

And then one night, I overheard the whispered conversation of my hosts which decided my destiny as a footpath dweller. It was a sultry night, and even in the verandah I had to constantly fan myself with a bit of cardboard, which I kept handy for the purpose.

"*Baap re! Kya garmi hai!*" (Oh, my father oh god, how hot it is!) I heard the wife say. "At least open the door and let some air come in."

"How can we keep the door open," the husband replied, "when he is sleeping there? It would be shameless for us."

And so the next day he—i.e., I—informed them that I had made arrangements for sleeping somewhere else.

"Are you sure you will be comfortable there?" the man asked with half-hearted politeness.

"Oh, yes," I lied, "it is a very big place." I could have added that it was as the city of Bombay.

The 1st Night: Beggar, My Neighbour!

"The first night on the footpath is the hardest, my friend," said my neighbour, the beggar, as he found me lying awake, uncomfortably turning and twisting.

How right he was: there was little sleep for me that night. The stones under me felt jagged with a thousand sharp edges all cutting into my flesh and bones. The open drain smelt of all the horrible odours imaginable. A mangy dog sniffed at my strange new face. A scrawny cat scurried over my legs, chasing a rat that only a moment ago was nibbling at my bare toes. I decided to put on my shoes and groped for them by my side. They were not there. They were gone. Stolen.

I looked up at the sky—the stars shone bright but far, very far from that footpath—and I had the frightening feeling that the high buildings were leaning over and might crash on me any moment.

A municipal refuse cart rumbled by. From the house above, some late-working housewife threw the day's cast-off food and vegetable peelings, some of them falling directly on me and the next moment all the neighbourhood dogs rushed to the spot, howling and barking and yelping at each other. On the main road, a car went by and I could hear the high-pitched laughter of girls—it seemed already to be from another world! A suburban train went clattering over a bridge somewhere nearby, so that the whole footpath vibrated with the thunderous rhythm of the wheels.

And through it all, the beggar, my neighbour, slept peacefully, oblivious to the odours and the sounds. How I envied him on that first night on the footpath!

57th Night: Guarding My Bank

I am already a veteran of the Footpath Brigade.

After the first night's experience, for some days I was choosy and finicky about the location of my bedroom.

I tried sleeping on a bench in the Hanging Gardens, at Chowpatty, with the cool sea-breeze to fan me, on the sea-wall at Marine Drive right in front of a famous film-star's flat, but I was chased and hounded out of all such fancy places by patrolling policemen—and so back to the Ferozeshah Mehta Road, in front of a bank. It gives me a peculiar feeling of security—as if the bank really belonged to me and I was sleeping there only to guard my property.

I always sleep with my face turned towards the high glass walls on which in golden letters is painted the name of the bank and the amount of its capital: ₹5,00,000,000! Now I am used to my "stony couch" and sleep quite comfortably and peacefully, but just before dozing off, I like to look at all those golden zeros, ₹5,00,000,000—5 crore, or is it 50 crore?—(my arithmetic was always weak) and thinking of all that money, I drift into sleep. Last night, I dreamt that I had got millions of rupees and was placing them end to end on the road so that they reached all the way from Bombay to my little town of Hathras in Uttar Pradesh, where my parents lived in the hope that one day their son would return with much money from Bombay…

127th Night: I shift to the Taj

I had to leave my bank after it was broken into by burglars. How well I remember the dramatic incidents of that night. The bank was fitted with an automatic alarm bell and when it started ringing, we were jerked out of our sleep, and we saw the burglars leaving in a hurry, and I was very angry as though it was my money that they were running off with… And so I grabbed one of the bandits by his trouser leg, and because he was carrying bundles of notes in both hands, he could not hit me without dropping the loot. But then as the police whistles sounded nearer, he gave me a violent kick and I was thrown back, still holding the burglar's trousers while he ran down the street, his shirt-tail flapping indecently in the air... I had a temptation to annex the excellent gabardine trousers, but like the good citizen that I am, I handed them over to the police. It was a valuable clue and I hoped to be rewarded. But when I gave my address as "Footpath in front of —Bank", they almost arrested me for complicity in the burglary, and after that I decided to keep away from banks. Maybe they aren't my banks, after all!

So I have shifted to the Taj Mahal Hotel—I mean the outer verandah where they provide excellent accommodation for unregistered guests like me. I have been clever enough to choose a spot from where I can enjoy the smell of the food in the ground floor restaurant and also have a glimpse of the guests arriving or departing late at night. Foreign Sahibs in black suits, Memsahibs in thin silk dresses revealing tantalising bits of their milk-white bodies, *khaddar*-clad leaders and their chiffon-clad ladies, rajas and ranis glittering with jewels, shining big, big cars rolling up, rolling away—"Ta-ta, my dear", "Bye-bye, my darling". It's a free show of wealth and fashion and beauty, more exciting than any film in a cinema, for those are only shadows, but here these beautiful Memsahibs are real.

Yes, it is much more exciting than the shadows of the screen. I can smell all the scents of their perfumed dresses, and once, as a young lady with a rather long skirt walked past me, I even got a touch of her dress on my face. Most disturbing, yet most pleasant. And the conversations one hears! As the late-night revellers come out in pairs after some drinks in the Permit Room, they are quite unmindful of us, mere vagrants, who lie in the verandah like lifeless corpses in the morgue. For them, we don't exist. Or, maybe, they know that we are there but they think we are asleep or that we don't understand English (little do they know about my school-leaving certificate and the BA degree of my friend Rajoo who also sleeps on the footpath); in any case, they talk freely in our presence, as if we do not matter.

"Come on, darling, please."

"But where? At this time of the night?"

"Let's drive down to Juhu—we can get a shack there." Then, in a mischievous whisper, "Or, if you like, there is the beach in the moonlight."

They depart in a burst of girlish giggles and manly laughter, and I lie there, my imagination aflame with visions of the moonlit Juhu beach, the palms softly waving in the breeze, and the hard stones under me are turned into soft, yielding sand, and I can feel the pressure of a youthful body against mine...

276th Night: When I Spoke to Dilip Kumar

It has been a long time since I left—or was obliged to leave—my "room" at the Taj. The guests were complaining of the unseemly sight of the vagrants who sprawled in the verandah, and so one night we were told to move off.

Since then, I have shifted several times from place to place, according to seasons. During the hot months before the monsoon I slept on Apollo Bunder; during the months of rain I slept in the wide, protected verandah of a big shop on Mahatma Gandhi Road, just in front of an illuminated shop-window displaying swimming costumes and brassieres. Again, a most disturbing neighbourhood! I am no longer without a job. I get ₹45 a month as a peon in an office—they call it "Import and Export" business, but I never see any goods coming or going; it's all done by letters and telegrams and telephone calls and hush-hush talks in the back rooms. I suspect it is some sort of black market business, But what do I care so long as I get my ₹45 a month?

I have a job, but still no roof over my head. For the dingiest *kholi* they demand a *pugree* of at least ₹200. I could, of course, move to one of those *bastis* in the suburbs where the South Indian building workers live in self-made thatched huts, but it would be too far from my place of work, and moreover, I like to be near the lights and the crowds and the traffic and the excitement of the city. I could also share a *kholi* with some other people—it would cost me only ₹10 a month—I even tried it for a night, but it was so hot in there, so hot, with six men with bad digestion snoring and belching in the little room without a window, that I ran back to my footpath under the open sky. I prefer the odours of the drain to the heat and the putrid smells of sweaty bodies in that room.

And so now I am here on Lamington Road, and even when I have no money to go to the pictures, I can get a free view of the crowds going in and out of all the cinemas lined up here, and on a premiere night, I can even see the stars in their big and beautiful cars. One day, I even got close enough to shout *"Arrey, wah, yaar"* to Dilip Kumar, but he didn't hear me clearly in all the noise and confusion and drove off without talking to me properly. But I will be moving again for I have just discovered that this place is too dangerously near the police stations.

537th Night: Under the Bridge

It has been getting chilly and I have moved again to take shelter under the Tilak Bridge. I have managed to acquire a canvas poster with a huge face of the beautiful Chanchalbala painted on it—it is so big that even her nose is one foot long—and when the cold breeze blows at night I cover myself with the canvas.

At first, I was decent enough to keep the painted side out, but then the vulgar-minded loafers would stop to look at the pretty face on my back and make indecent remarks and even draw a moustache above her beautiful lips. And so since then, I keep the unpainted side out, and embraced by the huge, beautiful face as I drift into sleep, my senses are assailed by a peculiarly fascinating smell—and I don't know whether it is the paint on the poster, or the perfumed powder on Miss Chanchalbala's face!

840th Night: The Flowers of Spring

Spring is here, even on the footpath. The leafless Gulmohar tree has suddenly blossomed with red flowers. When I look at them, I try to think out some deep philosophy—if my life is like this gaunt, leafless tree, then these flowers are…and then I give up. I am no footpath philosopher, like the beggar in that film who is always spouting words of wisdom that the dialogue-writer wrote for him.

But I know that spring is here. I like to look at the Gulmohar flowers, and I like to look at Champa, whose beauty is as startling and unexpected in this dismal world of the footpath-dwellers as those flaming red flowers in the leafless branches above.

I don't know where she has come from, but I know she is beautiful with pale-brown skin and big, black eyes, and shiny black hair that is like a living thing as it caresses her face and tumbles down her shoulders when she sits down to plait it with a broken-toothed comb. From my corner, I watch her, and so do all the others on our part of the footpath, but I know she has a special look for me, and it was no accident that we happened to go to the water tap at the same time, and while turning the tap, when my hand happened to touch hers, she didn't remove her hand; she even seemed to like it, or so I thought... or maybe it was all my imagination... For Champa is a good girl, not like so many others I have known—and some, more than known—in my years on the footpath. There is some deep sadness in those eyes, and also a bit of fear. Sometimes I think they look like the eyes of a hunted animal. But at other times, when she thinks no one is watching but I am looking at her from the corner of my eyes, I seem to see a softness creeping into those beautiful black eyes as her lips part in the faintest shadow of a smile, as if she was remembering something beautiful and tender from her past...

She speaks to no one, though every one has tried to make friendly overtures to her—some with patently evil motives. She has only one friend, a street dog whom she calls Moti—a starved, mangy creature with one broken leg—and it is difficult to imagine how one so beautiful could love such an ugly animal. But on the footpath, one sees and experiences many strange things, and so we come to accept the strange silent girl and her dog as a part of our strange existence.

No one knows that Champa does in the daytime. But everyday when I return from work, I have an uncomfortable feeling in the pit of my stomach, a nameless fear that she might have gone away, but then I see her there, talking to her dog, and I feel limp with relief and thanksgiving and happiness. I seem to be living only for that one moment.

At night, when we all spread our rags and bits of paper on the footpath to prepare our "beds", many sly attempts are made to move closer to Champa's corner—especially by Raghia, who has the body of a wrestler, and Bansi, who is thin like a reed and always chewing *paan* and humming film songs. But Champa is more than adequately guarded by her dog, who starts barking madly if someone makes the slightest movement towards her. Last night, it almost tore off a piece of Raghia's leg, though he kept on protesting that he was only going to the tap to drink water.

907th Night: A Man, a Girl, and a Dog

Tonight I am so happy that I cannot sleep.

Tonight Champa talked to me—for the first time. When I came back at night, I found the footpath deserted. I remembered that it was the night of Diwali and that our fellow-lodgers must have gone to see the lights, to pickpocket in the conveniently overcrowded streets, to beg for alms and get free sweets from the temples. But Champa was there as usual, and she was washing the dog.

I dared not make the first move to break the ice, but I coughed aloud and dusted off my bit of *chatai* to announce my arrival.

"*Arrey*, Moti," she addressed the dog, "are you not going to see the lights?"

The dog shook his wet head, throwing off a spray of water, but I know the question was for me. Still I dared not speak.

"Maybe you are afraid of the crowds? There will be so many people in the streets. You may get trampled or run over."

This time I spoke. "You are right, Champa. I hate crowds—I feel so lonely in crowds."

She expected me to answer her, yet she was startled when I did speak.

Then she got up and said to the dog—and to me, "Come, let's go and see the lights—but, mind you, we shall keep away from the crowds."

The man, the girl and the dog—this strange procession tramped the streets, and I could see the million lights reflected in Champa's eyes, which looked at the them with girlish wonder. Still we did not talk, except a few words spoken through the dog. On our way back, as we were passing a big store, Champa paused for a moment before the lit-up shop window, looking at the beautiful saris and glittering jewellery displayed there. I could see her face reflected in the glass, and I saw in her eyes a fleeting look of desire, as if she desperately wanted all those things and the life of comfort and security that they represented.

And I wanted to cry out, "Oh, Champa, Champa, I want to give you these silk saris and these jewels—all the beautiful things of the world, for you are beautiful yourself and deserve everything that is good and beautiful. I want to give you a home of your own, children of your own, if only you would speak to me…"

But she spoke only to the dog and said, "Come, Moti, let's go home."

Home! That's what she called that corner of the footpath, that bundle of rags, those earthen pots in which she cooked her food. If only I could give her a real home!

And now, as I write this in the light of the street lamp, I can see Champa sleeping there in her corner, guarded by her ever-vigilant Moti. She is beautiful in her sleep, and on her lips is a gentle smile, as if she was dreaming a dream of happiness. Could it be that I am in this smiling dream of hers?

943th Night: Great News For Us

We who live on the footpath are indifferent to politics, plans, projects, budgets, because they seem to be completely unrelated to our life. Newspapers interest us only as material to spread on our beds of stones and, sometimes, even to cover us when it gets chilly at night.

But this morning, as I got up, I saw something in the newspaper on which I had been sleeping which greatly interested and even excited me. The headline was "Homes for the Homeless"—and the news was about the Government's plan to build many thousand little houses for homeless people with small incomes. I tore up that bit from the paper, carefully folded it and kept it in my pocket next to my heart. I felt greatly warmed by it, and went about my work in a gay mood the whole day, and my boss had to warn me about whistling in the office.

In the evening, I hurried to the footpath even without having my meal, and was lucky to find Champa alone, talking to her dog.

"Look, Champa"—today I ventured to talk to her directly—"Here is great news for you." And I took out the bit of newspaper and gave it to her.

She shook her head and said, "I cannot read. Tell me what it says."

"It says that our Government is building houses for people like us who sleep on the footpaths." I went on speaking excitedly, "Isn't it wonderful, Champa? We are going to have our own homes. Then we shall not have to sleep on the footpath. Then we—I mean, you and me—don't you understand, Champa?"

She nodded her head to say that she did understand and then, with a sad little smile that was a sigh as well as a smile, she asked, "But when?"

So I had to read the bit of news all over again and I found that it said that though the work on these houses would begin soon, it was calculated that it would take at least 10 years to provide a roof for every one of the homeless millions.

My optimism and enthusiasm of the morning has been dampened a little, but still I am not despondent. I am only hoping that when these new houses begin to be allotted, our turn—mine and Champa's—may come soon, for now my thoughts are set on marriage, on children, and one cannot raise a family without a roof over one's head.

976th Night: A Glimpse of Our Home

Tonight I am happy beyond words, and even Champa seems to be coming out of her shell of sadness. As I write this, she is humming a song as she cooks her food—I can recognise the song, too. It is a song that women in her part of the country sing on the occasion of marriage. Everyone on the footpath is surprised at her new mood, but I am not surprised, for I know the reason for her happy mood.

I am happy, too, because today I took her to see the house in which we are going to live in the future. Already we know what it is going to look like.

It happened like this. Not far from our footpath, for the last several days, there has been a blaze of lights and a blaring of loudspeakers so it is difficult for us to sleep. It is an exhibition and the sign at the entrance reads: "Five-Year Plan".

Now, as I have already noted earlier in the diary, generally we footpath-dwellers do not care much for plans and projects. But the words "Five-Year Plan" rung a bell in my heart, for in that bit of newspaper which was still kept safely in my pocket, the building of those "Homes for the Homeless" was mentioned as a part of the Second Five-Year Plan.

So I drifted along with the crowd into the exhibition. There were many wonderful things there, and many charts and diagrams that I did not understand, but there was one thing which drew me like a magnet, and I stood before it, fascinated. Then I ran back to the footpath and, disregarding the puzzled and even scandalised looks of my neighbours, I boldly caught Champa by the hand and dragged her to the exhibition.

"Look, Champa, that's our house," I shouted as we reached the model of a two-room house. The descriptive card read: "Such houses will be built for people who have no homes."

It was but a model, but we stood there and looked longingly and lovingly at it, for it seemed like all our dreams come true—a room, a kitchen, a verandah, a tree in the courtyard, and under the tree, dolls representing three happy children! It was too beautiful for words, and we were speechless with wonder. When we returned, I saw that there were tears of happiness in Champa's eyes.

Now she is asleep, and the smile on her beautiful sleeping face is the smile of hope and deep contentment.

978th Night: The Death of a Friend

Something has happened which has shattered the spell of happiness that we—Champa and I—had known since we saw that house in the exhibition.

Moti died today, poisoned by someone, and from the look of triumph on Raghia's face, I suspect the evil deed is his.

Champa is like a lost soul. She sat with the dead dog in her arms for a long time, tears silently flowing from her eyes, then she got up and carried her beloved Moti as a bereaved father carries his dead child to the place of burial. I wanted to go with her but she gave me a pleading look as if to say, "Please! Let me be alone with my burden of sorrows." I respected her need of being alone and remained where I was.

After an hour, she returned, having disposed of the remains of her pet. Now there were no tears in her eyes, but a grim, ominous, dry-eyed silence that was frightening. I tried to comfort her and even said, "Champa, come, eat something." She did not reply, only giving me a look of surprise which plainly said, "Can I eat when my poor Moti is dead?" And I knew it was no use insisting.

Raghia, boastful and arrogant with his bulging muscles, said aloud, "Why, Champa, who will guard you at night now? Maybe you could keep me instead of the dog." He laughed at his own unseemly joke, no one joined him. As for Champa, she only turned her face towards him for a moment; there was such cold contempt in her eyes that the wave of laughter froze on Raghia's face and he turned it into embarrassed coughing. Then she collected her bundle of rags and moved away from whole group, making her bed on the very edge of the pavement. She lay down there, but I could see that she was not sleeping, but looking up at the stars. I must keep awake, too, for now that Moti is gone, who else is there to protect her innocence from the evil intentions of men like Raghia?

989th Night: Picture of a Dream

Time is a great healer, and slowly, Champa seems to be overcoming the grief of the death of her dog. Tonight, as I returned from work, she even greeted me with a smile—a pale, wan smile but a smile all the same.

I had brought her a gift—the picture of that dream house of ours, which we had seen in the exhibition, which I had cut out of a magazine in our office. I gave it to her, and was glad to see a sparkle of interest in her eyes as she recognised it. She said, "May I keep it?" and when I said, "Yes, of course—I brought it for you," she looked at me with those child-like eyes of hers full of gratitude.

Tonight, after many days, she is sleeping peacefully. The last tram has rattled past us by. The University clock tower chimes the hour of two, and I feel sleepy, too...

990th Night: The House Collapses

I never knew that in one night—in a few moments, indeed—the world can come to an end, and all one's hopes, all one's dreams, come crashing down like... Last night, I went to sleep shortly after two in the morning. I drifted into a peaceful dream. I dreamt that I and Champa had shifted to our own house, that there was a fire burning in our kitchen, a pot of rice on the stove, that the tree in the compound was aflame with red Gulmohar flowers and that under the tree our three children—two boys and one girl—were playing. And then suddenly, as it happens in dreams, without a warning or reason, there was a storm, there were flashes of lightning and thunder which shook our little house. I had a sudden fearful premonition, for a vicious tongue of lightning was reaching out for the chimney of our house, and I knew that Champa was in the kitchen, cooking food for us. The next moment, before I could shout a warning, lightning struck our house with a deafening roar, which was strangely like a car dashing against a wall, a shattering of glass-panes, and a vicious, whining, screeching of brakes... I got up with a start and found the footpath in turmoil. Everyone seemed to be in a panic. A smashed-up car was halfway up the wall, its wheels still viciously revolving in the air, and dripping from them something dark and thick—blood! Champa's blood!

I rushed to where she lay, her body ground to pulp by the heavy car—but her face was untouched and on her lips was the same gentle smile as if she was still seeing some beautiful, happy dream, and in her tightly clutched hand there was something—the picture of our dream-house!

The owner-driver of the car was found to be only slightly injured as the people pulled him out of the car. A young man in a white coat and black trousers, he smelt of whisky and was muttering, "Damn shame that my steering wheel broke, but why must these people sleep on the footpath?" And I briefly thought I would tell him why, but I had no voice left, no strength except to see and to hear. And when the police came and asked him for his name and address, I heard him give a number on Malabar Hill.

"Flat number?" the policeman asked.

And the young man replied, "The whole building belongs to us."

Now Champa is gone in flames and only a stain of her blood remains on the footpath, and I lie here on a newspaper which prints the good news that the Government of Bombay has built a beautiful dormitory to accommodate the footpath-dwellers.

1000th Night: Now We are only 19,999!

I am writing this—probably the last entry in this diary—at the unusual hour of four in the morning. After 10 nights of wakefulness, tortured by the memory of Champa, I had just drifted into a fitful slumber when I was rudely awakened by the voice of authority.

They were some policemen and some social workers.

They said they were making a census of the footpath dwellers.

One of them told me that now there are only 20,000 people sleeping on the pavements—and I told him that he could further reduce this number by one. Since Champa's death, there must be only 19,999 sleeping on these beds of stones.

They asked me why I preferred to sleep on the footpath, when for five *annas* a night I could sleep in the municipal dormitory.

They tell me how clean and comfortable that building is. I know it already, for I have been to the dormitory—its airy, lighted rooms are palaces compared to the stink and discomfort of the footpath. I have seen the bathrooms where one can really bathe, I have seen the dining room and the beautiful little theatre where the homeless will sing and dance to entertain themselves.

"So why don't you sleep there?" They cross-examined me. "Can't you afford even five *annas* a day?"

I tell them I earn more than a rupee a day.

"Then why don't you sleep there? Why? Why? Why?? WHY???" The questions overwhelm me. I want to answer, but I have no voice, no way of expressing myself. I am afraid they will not understand me.

I want to tell them that the dormitory is a wonderful place, very cheap at five *annas* a night. But I don't want to sleep in a dormitory, with other people in the same room. A kitchen, a little garden with a Gulmohar tree with its red flowers, for me and my Champa and our three children… They go away at last, thinking I am mentally unsound. And I sit here in the light of the street lamp writing my diary, and not far from me on the footpath is the stain of blood, which is all that remains of Champa and her dreams.

Soon, the rains will be here and even this stain will be washed away. Then what shall remain of my Champa and me?

And so ends the record of my one thousand nights on this bed of stones!

P.S. I don't know who makes all those wonderful plans and projects. If any of them reads these lines, I want to ask him to hurry up with those houses if they really want to save me and my Champa and our three children that will never be born!

DEATH OF AN EMPEROR

The Emperor was overworked and old. Unknown to his engineers and mechanics, "he" had developed an insidious growth which was, indeed, cancer of the metal. The Emperor's bones creaked and protested every time "he" landed and took off. It was like an arthritic old man who had cancer of the bones.

But all this was the inside story, never revealed to anyone—except when it was too late! Outwardly, "The Emperor Ashoka" was still the pride of Air India's fleet of jumbo jets. Its interior had an eye catching beauty and its comforts were all that any tourist could expect, and its First Class was a class by itself. The air hostesses, in their rustling silks, were like sleek Greek goddesses who flitted about, walking the aisles, distributing their imperious smiles to all the passengers. Its flight pursers, perfectly moulded in their form-fitting uniform of shirt and slacks walked about with indifferent elegance, performing their chores with efficiency and ease.

The Emperor was proud of his special boudoir called the "Maharaja's Lounge". Its brocade draperies lent it an Oriental splendour and glamour that was irresistible to any man or woman. Accessible through a winding carpeted staircase, it had all the affluent air of a mini pent house—and more!

"WELCOME" was painted on the steps of the Emperor that led to the interior of the jumbo jet. Ramoo whistled as he climbed up the stairs, holding the embarkation card in his left hand, while his right hand gripped what looked like a parcel of books tied in dirty old newspapers with a thick coir rope.

"What are you carrying in this parcel?" the police officer, making a perfunctory check at the airport, had asked him.

"Currency notes, Sir," he had said—and then laughed at his own joke.

"Such jokes will land you in trouble, young man," the police officer had said.

"Sorry, sir," he had hastened to apologise and his fingers had slid the knots of the rope, "If you want the truth—these are religious books worth their weight in gold!"

The police officer had declined the young man's offer to untie the parcel because he knew that every time he undid a parcel, he had to repack it just as neatly and that took time. And there was no time. The plane was already 10 hours late and he had spent nearly two minutes on this young man and his shabby parcel. Religious books? They must be volumes of the Ramayana and the Bhagwad Gita and the Vedas. At this rate, it would take him six hours to clear all the passengers, supposedly nearly 200 that day. He shuddered at the thought of how much time it would have taken him had the plane been carrying its full load of over 300 passengers! His New Year's Eve would have been reduced to a 12-hour working shift which would have ended in the early hours of the next morning.

Ramoo heaved a sigh of relief in the air-conditioned interior of the Emperor and whistled again, this time to express his appreciation of the statuesque body of the air hostess, who turned round at his whistle and gave him her unperturbable smile.

As he found his window seat at the rear of the long cabin, he dumped the heavy parcel at his feet and gave himself up to contemplation.

"I have given the slip to those jokers—Akhtar and Johnny. After all, I did the dirty work. What makes them think I will give them one-third of my money?"

Ramoo, Akhtar and Johnny were known in the underworld of Bombay as Amar, Akbar and Anthony—because they always worked together and were thick as thieves—or as blood brothers!

In "Operation Dubai", it was true that the bank robbery was Ramoo's idea and he had executed it with his usual finesse and good luck. But the passport that would take him to Dubai had been forged by Akhtar, who operated a passport and visa racket—otherwise known as the Global Employment Agency. And Johnny had invested his hard cash—for which he had committed sacrilege and robbed a church—in one ticket to Dubai for Ramoo. In return, Ramoo had promised them one-third of whatever he would get out of the bank. But then, he had not expected to get such a large booty as he had. Several lakh rupees are several lakh rupees. He could put it in a Dubai bank and then become a full-fledged smuggler. He could return to India as a "respectable" businessman who had made his pile in the Middle East. So why should he give two-thirds of his luck to those loafers? After all, he would send them ₹5,000 each—that would take care of the passport and the air ticket!

At this point of thought, he looked up and saw his worst misgivings take shape in the hefty form of Akhtar Nawaz Khan coming down the aisle, being shown to a seat on the other side, two rows ahead of him. "How could this fellow get a passport and visa so quickly?" He thought, forgetting that it was Akhtar's handiwork that had provided him his own passport and visa!

More and more people were coming in now and Ramoo thought he would be well-hidden from Akhtar behind the protective screen of a dozen *mazdoors*—masons and brick-layers with their tin trunks and shabby clothes, wide-eyed at the prospect of going to Dubai, the El Dorado or *jannat* (for these were Muslims, undoubtedly), the land where rivers of gold and silver flowed down to the sea! But he felt someone's coat lightly brush against him as he sat down besides him, aggressively familiar. Ramoo turned to look and was petrified to find Johnny Gonsalves, his erstwhile partner whom he had double-crossed.

"Hi, Ramoo, where do you think you are going?" He spoke in a loud tone, despite Ramoo's efforts at hushing him.

"Hello, Johnny," Ramoo's voice came out in a squeak. "I am sorry I could not keep that appointment. I was in a hurry, you see how it is!"

"Yes, I can see that you were in hell of a hurry to get away with half-a-million rupees!"

"Shush!" Ramoo turned to silence him. But his caution was unnecessary because most of the passengers who had taken their seats in their vicinity did not understand any English and even if they did have a smattering of it, they could not make head or tale of what they were saying!

Ramoo's hand was protectively touching his parcel of "books" when he felt it being taken away from him. It was Johnny who was grabbing it with a confidence that was unnerving.

"Come on, cry out! Or snatch it away from my hand. Raise an alarm. Make a hue and cry. Do something, damn it!"

The plane was now full—there were plenty of vacant seats all round—so Johnny took the bundle across the aisle to the seat next to Akhtar.

"So both the bastards have joined hands to rob me of my money," Ramoo thought.

Then he saw the air hostess coming down the aisle, going straight to Johnny.

"I am sorry, you can't sit here!"

"Why?" answered Johnny, "Why can't I sit here with my friend?"

"Because it will disturb the equilibrium of the plane!" she said, "The flight is about to take off. The passengers have been equally divided on both sides of the aisle. You will upset the balance of the plane by sitting here. Please go back to your seat. Look, that passenger over there is calling you."

Johnny reluctantly eased himself out of the seat and, leaving his parcel behind with Akhtar, went back to the seat next to the scowling Ramoo.

"Welcome home, 'Sir'," taunted Ramoo, then turned to the air hostess and said, "My friend has forgotten his parcel over there."

The air hostess took two strides and picked it up before Akhtar could say anything.

She dumped the parcel on the empty seat beside Johnny and went back after admonishing both the passengers, "Fasten your seat belts, please."

As they were fastening their seat belts, scowling at each other and eyeing the parcel, the plane began to taxi. The bulky Emperor lumbered down the runway to the starting point, creaking at the joints like an arthritic old man.

Here, the engines developed maximum power while the lights were dimmed in the cabin.

"Ladies and gentlemen," came the Captain's voice in perfect English, "the lights are being put out, so that you can enjoy the lights of Bombay. You can put on the reading lights if you are afraid of the dark."

The reading light was already on, and falling on the parcel. Johnny extended his hand and switched it off.

"Didn't you hear what the Captain said?" asked Ramoo.

"Yes, I did. That's why I switched it off. I am not afraid of the dark. What would you prefer? A knife in your ribs? Or a drop of cyanide mixed in your cold drink?"

"What is sy-nide?" asked Ramoo.

"It is quite painless. One moment you are alive and the next moment you are dead."

To make himself understood, he had to shout above the roar of the engines. The plane was picking up speed for take-off. The next moment, they were off the ground.

Johnny put his hand where the parcel was. His hand came down on the empty seat. The parcel was gone.

"It's gone" Johnny cried aloud.

"Serves you right! Stealing other people's money. Then threatening to kill them !"

Johnny was exasperated, and his hands reached out to the neck of Ramoo.

But all the lights in the cabin were immediately switched on. His hands remained frozen in the pre-strangling posture. The air-hostess was coming towards them.

"What's it?" she enquired of them. Her tone was one of annoyance, as if two boys had been discovered fighting in the plane.

"Nothing," Johnny, suddenly realising the implication of his frozen hands, said, "We were just playing a game."

"You gave me a fright!" she said, "I thought you were going to strangle him."

"He was," Ramoo said to her, then added, as an afterthought, "playing a game."

"Then don't do it again" she warned them, "or someone might take you seriously." Then she retreated, her high heels making a soft clicking sound on the carpet on the aisle.

Ramoo produced a clasp Rampuri knife from his pocket and playfully clicked it open. The blade flashed menacingly in the light.

"If you had touched me," said Ramoo, as if having a casual conversation, "this knife would have pierced your guts." Then he just as cleverly and casually closed the knife but held it in his hand, his thumb on the lever that would click it open. "So we better not play any games," he added, "and jointly think of how to retrieve the money from that *musalla*, Akhtar."

Johnny had no time to think of where the parcel had gone. Then he looked ahead across the aisle to where Akhtar was sitting and found him grinning back at him.

Akhtar made the "thumbs-up" sign to him to indicate that all was well.

"Don't worry," Akhtar shouted back at him, "It's safer with me up to the Dubai customs."

Johnny remembered the arrangement he had made with Akhtar when they realised they had been double-crossed a few hours before the flight. They had no difficulty in arranging tickets. There had been so many cancellations that the Airlines people were glad to add two more passengers to the remaining list. Akhtar had suggested that the Dubai customs people knew him and wouldn't open his parcel, whatever it contained. Johnny, being on his first visit, would be more suspect. So the parcel had to be carried out by Akhtar. Johnny, recalling all this, relaxed in his seat, even closed his eyes to ease the tension of the last few seconds.

He felt someone jumping over his knees. It was Ramoo. He was striding along the aisle, going to Akhtar, and the next moment, he was engaged in a struggle with Akhtar over the parcel. They both pulled at the strings until it snapped and bundles of currency notes fell on the floor.

Their scuffle to retrieve the bundles of notes upset the equilibrium of the Emperor and the plane, not having gained sufficient height, tilted dangerously.

The air hostess ran in alarm, shouting at both of them, "You are upsetting the equilibrium of the plane.

Go back to your seats." As they returned, she saw bundles of notes on the aisle. When she bent on her knees, she saw Ramoo picking up the bundles of notes.

"This money is mine," he cried, hysterically.

"I don't care whose it is," she shouted back, picking up some bundles, "but you are upsetting the balance of the plane, endangering the lives of all the passengers."

The plane was tilting to the other side now. The Captain was mystified. Why was the plane tilting, first to one side, then to the other? They were also losing height rapidly.

Ramoo had managed to pick up some more bundles of notes from the aisle, while the others were picked up by Akhtar, who just extended his hands.

"Please keep your seat belts fastened. We are losing height dangerously," came the Captain's voice over the Intercom. There was panic among the passengers; the warning was translated by the ones who knew English for those who didn't.

The next moment, three mad men—Ramoo, Akhtar and Johnny, or Amar Akbar and Anthony—were chasing each other all over the plane, snatching the bundles of notes from each other, and every time they were on one side, the plane tilted dangerously to that side, till they went on the other side and then the huge plane tilted dangerously on that side.

The passengers watched this dangerous comedy with petrified faces. Even the air hostesses were dumbfounded, unable to check the three greedy men who were endangering the lives of 180 men, women and children.

A child began to cry—

A woman was weeping—

Older men were remembering the names of their gods—

The next moment, the old Emperor had hit the water —there was an explosion—and the currency notes fell from the lifeless hands of Amar, Akbar and Anthony.

The old and ailing Emperor, with 180 passengers and a crew of 24, went down like a lump of diseased metal. Nobody would ever know what brought about the end of the Emperor—was it a time-bomb? Was something wrong with the metal, eaten into by cancer? Or was it the scuffle of the three mad, greedy, young men who were chasing each other in the half-empty plane, tilting it, now this way and now that, before it had ascended to a safe height? No one would ever know.

One little fish swallowed the bottle of cyanide and died instantly.

One big fish swallowed the poisoned fish and also died, though not so quickly.

A medium-sized fish swallowed a swollen lump that was sometime ago a bundle of currency notes and it stuck in the fish's throat till it died of suffocation. It would never know that it had died of a human disease known as Money.

THE GUN

(For Smita Patil)

The Gun was lying on the ground and, in the excitement of that split second, saying something to him. It was reminding him of certain things and events.

His whole life flashed through his mind in that moment—his motherless childhood, his attachment to his poor father, who had died a pauper. His first awareness of being a Harijan and his knowledge that Harijans were really Untouchables. He recollected all the things that he had held in his hands as a child—the three-wheel walker, the toy plough, the reed pen, the *khurpee* and the real plough. The Gun (which he now snatched up) was the climax of his life's dreams, starting with the *gadelna* as the three-wheeled walker was called in his village. What was *he* called in his childhood? The child's name was Rudloo Ram but everyone called him Munna. He learnt to use his little legs with the help of a *gadelna* which his father's carpenter friend had made especially for him. The little wheels, fashioned on the circular saw, were dyed with lacquer. The child was fascinated by the red colour. It was a game and a school of learning for him. Learning to walk—that was life for him. Movement, walking, running, falling, getting Up—all facets of life were represented in this game!

When he learnt to walk, he tired of the three-wheeled walker. Now the motherless son of the peasant needed a new game. So his uncle, Ram Deen, gave him a different toy on Diwali time. It was no ordinary toy: a miniature model of a plough, like the one with which his father tilled his half-acre of land and carried on his shoulders, going to the fields before sunrise and returning at dusk along with the cows, which were coming back from the pasture. When the child got the toy plough, he forgot the Walker. Now he wanted to plough the land like his father. When he set out for the fields the next morning, he followed him with his little plough on his shoulder. When Raghoo tied the pair of oxen to the plough, dug the blade into the soft earth and used the rope to incite the oxen to move, the child would also imitate his father by digging the earth with the miniature blade of his plough. As his father scattered the seed with his hand, so the son would imitate him by scattering a handful of dust picked up from the field!

When he grew up a little, his father took him to the village school and persuaded the teacher to admit him in Class One. Harijan children were admitted because the school got a grant from the Government on that condition, but they were seated in the open, under a tree where they could not pollute the boys of the upper castes. They had their own pitcher of water, which always contained tepid water because it was kept in the sun. For school, Munna got a special gift from his father—a pen made out of a reed. The pen was a new kind of toy, and to possess it gave a new sense of pride to Rudloo. He felt a strange sense of pleasure—and power!—by holding it in his hand.

One day, he drank water out of the pitcher of water meant only for the upper castes. Disgusted by the lukewarm water of the Harijans' pitcher, he was tempted by the cool look of the wet mud pitcher, which had a tumbler placed on top of it. A Brahmin boy saw him taking water from the pitcher he was not supposed to touch and raised an alarm. That created a furore in the whole school.

The teacher first gave a few slaps to Rudloo, then turned him out of the school because the Harijan boy refused to accept his mistake. He argued angrily with his teacher: why could he not drink water from that pitcher?

"Because you are an untouchable—an *achhoot*!" the teacher retorted angrily.

Rudloo knew his father's caste was Harijan but this was the first time that he had heard himself called an *achhoot*.

He said, "No, Master*ji*. You are wrong. We are not *achhoot*. We are Harijans by caste."

"*Arrey*, Harijan and *achhoot* have the same meaning," said the teacher, "Gandhi*ji*, by giving you the name of Harijan, has turned your heads. Run off from here. And don't you come to school again!"

Rudloo was in a temper. He threw his books, notebooks, slate and wooden *takhtee* into the dust. In the end, he was left with the pen which his father had made for him. He was just about to throw it on the ground when he desisted, as if the pen was saying something to him. "I am a very useful thing. Don't throw me away. One day, you will regret it."

He wondered, "How can a lifeless pen speak?" And he threw the pen away. The tip of the pen was soaked in ink. Where it fell, it made a blot on the ground—a blot which looked just like a flower!

But Rudloo, at that time, was not in a mood for flowers. His feet deliberately trampled that ink-flower. As he stamped it, he heard—or thought he heard—the cry of a child.

Let the child cry, he thought, and angrily walked away. Walking through the village, he arrived in Harijan *wadi,* where the lanes were unpaved, where the gutter of dirty waters flowed in the middle of the "road", where there was mud and filth every where, where worms wriggled in the puddles of dirty water, and where the well was also *kachcha.* It had no *pakka* parapet wall round it and Rudloo had, several times, just escaped falling into the well. All that, he had seen before. But that day, they assumed a new significance and relevance to his life—the life of every Harijan or *achhoot.*

He had already thrown away the pen and he told his father defiantly that he would never go to school again. His father handed him a *khurpee* instead of a pen, and taught him how to use it to cut grass. There was a lot of grass growing wild around their hut. Wielding the *khurpee,* he cut and collected a pile of grass which he hauled to the market place and there sold it to a *syce* who had come there to buy grass for his horse. The groom gave him two 10-paise coins and asked him to bring the same amount of grass every day. The next day, when he went to cut the grass, his hand wielded the *khurpee* expertly and with greater speed. Now he was enjoying working with the *khurpee,* which he had never done while writing with the pen. That day he cut more grass and sold the pile for 30 paise, which proved that the *khurpee* was better—and more useful—than the pen. The pen had not helped him earn even a single paisa.

So, for many years, Rudloo kept on plying the *khurpee* and selling grass. The grass, in the meantime, had also become more expensive. Now he could sell it for 50 paise. But everything—the rice, the *dal* and the oil—that he had to buy with the coins he got from selling grass had also become dearer.

His father continued to plough the land.

When Rudloo grew up, he realised the poor peasant's plight, the misery of a peasant's existence. Every year, after harvest time, his father would borrow money from the *sahukar* to buy the seed for the next crop. Every year, he planned to pay off the debt at the time of the next harvest. But the next harvest, too, he had to sell to the same *sahukar*, who paid him so little for it that, with great difficulty, he managed to pay the interest while the principal remained unpaid and accumulated. By the time the next year drew to an end, the interest had to be paid all over again.

One year, there was such a drought that there was no water in the well. The crop withered away and Rudloo could not earn anything because all the grass had first yellowed, then dried up, and died! That year, when he could not pay even the interest, Rudloo's father had to mortgage their land to the *sahukar*. "Now this land no longer belongs to us," said his father, "This belongs to the *sahukar*." Rudloo felt as if the ground had slipped under his feet.

First, the land was mortgaged to the money-lender.

Two years later, the land had to be sold to the same *sahukar.*

Now, Raghoo and his son, Rudloo, had to work on their land—which they could not call their own any more—as landless labourers. The owner was the *sahukar* who now came to possess many of their neighbours' pieces of land, too. Raghoo and Rudloo stood in the sun the whole day—ploughing, sowing, watering, pruning—and then, when the crop stood high, harvesting it and handing over the whole crop to the *sahukar.* Only then would he condescend to give them half a maund of grain. Now their condition was reduced to that of slaves.

Then Raghoo fell ill and Rudloo had to do the work of two in the field which once was theirs but now belonged to the *sahukar*. Again, he had to go to the same *sahukar* to ask for a loan.

"Sign here," said the *sahukar*, putting forward a blank paper, "or put your thumb impression. Who knows when the old man will die. Now you have to take over his responsibilities. Let the son place his thumb impression!" he told his clerk. While his thumb was being smeared with ink, Rudloo realised the importance of the pen he had once thrown away. He could neither read nor write. He did not know what figure the clerk had written or would write later on the blank paper on which he had to put his thumb impression.

While fixing his thumb on the paper, Rudloo felt as if his thumb was being cut off. He knew then that he was no more than a slave of the *sahukar*.

The next month, despite the medicines he had bought with the money he had borrowed from the *sahukar*, his father died. The last rites had to be performed and the whole *biradari* had to be fed and feasted. So Rudloo again had to go to the *sahukar*. Again, he had to put his thumb impression. He was getting used to the procedure.

During one year, he had to put his thumb impression on five or six different papers.

One night, only four months ago, he saw some of the young landless labourers stealing out of the village.

"Where are you all going like thieves?" he asked one of them.

His friend told him that they were going to hear a revolutionary leader of landless peasants like them speak. Rudloo tagged along with them. He did not even know what was "Revolutionary" and what was "revolution". But he sensed a strange stirring in his heart every time he heard either word—"revolutionary" or "revolution"!

When they arrived in a mango grove in the neighbouring village, he saw, in the light of a torch that was burning there, the revolutionary leader who was just like him—dark and slim but tough-bodied. But he had big black eyes in which a fire seemed to be smouldering. Nobody knew the Revolutionary's name. He was only called "Comrade". Rudloo thought this was his name—till he addressed them all, "Comrades. Any questions before I speak?"

"*Kamred*," Rudloo savoured the name on his tongue for the first time as he put up his hand, "What is meant by *inquilab*?"

"*Inquilab* is the great turning-over," the young leader, who was called just "Comrade", replied. "When the sky comes down to the earth and the earth goes up to the sky, those who are called 'lowly' go on the top and those who are on top come tumbling down!"

Rudloo liked the sound of the word "revolution"—the great turning-over!

"What should we do to bring about *inquilab*?" was Rudloo's next question.

"Take up the Gun!" came the reply, and at that point it seemed to him as if the Gun was saying, "Nothing can be achieved without power. And power comes out of the barrel of a Gun!"

Rudloo could not understand this. He asked, "From where shall we get the Gun?"

"When the time comes, the Gun, of its own accord, will come into your hands. You may not have a Gun today but your enemies will certainly have a lot of Guns."

Then he elaborated on the theme of how landless labourers had to be mobilised to fight for their rights. "Demand at least four rupees a day for your work," he told them. "Whatever this Government has fixed for you is the lowest wage."

Rudloo was not concentrating on all this; his mind was still toying with the idea of the Gun. When the big-eyed youth was going away, he turned to Rudloo and his companions and Rudloo felt it was he whom he was addressing.

"When the Gun falls into your hands, come over that hill beyond this village. There you will meet us. We are living in the jungle beyond that! There we rule. That is *our* territory."

The Comrade (who had no other name) took his Gun, and, slinging it on his shoulder, strode into the darkness, leaving Rudloo with a lot of vague ideas. What did the Comrade mean by his words?

The next day, he was working in the field (which once was his father's but now belonged to the *sahukar*) when the *sahukar* arrived there to ensure that the labourers were working properly. He was accompanied by a tall, hefty man who looked like a villain he had once seen in a picture when the touring talkies had come to their village. In his hands, he had a Gun!

"Did the *Kamred* mean that we should snatch away this Gun?" he thought to himself.

But the *sahukar* went away after some time.

That "villain" also went with him.

The Gun also "walked" away with the villain.

But the Gun obsessed Rudloo's mind. At night, he even dreamt of snatching away the Gun from that man's hands. But the man, apprehending Rudloo, aimed and fired at him. The bullet hit him in the heart…and Rudloo got up in a cold sweat.

He got up to drink water but there was not even a drop in the water-pot in his house. So he went to the *kuchcha* well in *Harijan wadi,* but that well, he remembered, had dried up. There was nothing but mud at the bottom of it. The only source of water for the Harijans was to walk a couple of miles to the town's railway station, where the water tank arrived on the morning train and each of them could get one pitcher of water. But his thirst was demanding water now, in the middle (or end) of the night!

He thought of the *pukka* well in their village. Why shouldn't he bring water from it? At that hour, there would be no one there! It was only half a mile away and soon he was at the well, pulling the bucket with half the rope slung over the *charkhi*. He was about to pull the bucket towards him when the Brahmin village priest, muttering his prayers, happened to arrive there and reacted as if he had seen not a man but a ghost. Then he realised that it was a Harijan youth.

"You scoundrel! You dare to come here and pollute the whole well by putting your dirty bucket and your rope with it. Your *biradari* will have to pay for the whole cleansing ceremony which will cost several hundred rupees!"

The priest continued to shout and complain.

Rudloo did not speak a word and walked away with the bucket full of water. When he returned to his *wadi*, he told his neighbours, "I have bought this water to drink from the *pukka* well and the village priest has seen me. Now he wants to impose a collective fine on all of us."

The warning was delivered in the evening.

"Either give ₹150 for the collective fine or prepare for the consequences."

The Harijan *khet mazdoors* were defiant. They replied, "Today, only Rudloo came; tomorrow, all of us will come to the well with our buckets and our pots. We will see who dares to stop us."

That night, there was a fire in the *Harijan wadi*.

It was not an accidental fire. The upper caste *lathials* had brought burning torches to set fire to the Harijans' huts.

But the *lathials* were armed. In one hand, they carried flaming torches, in the other, they had guns.

Rudloo woke up with a start when the walls and roof of his hut were already in flames. Still, he risked his life and jumped out of the fire.

His *dhoti* caught fire, singeing his hair and burning his left leg. He was just letting one of his neighbours put out the fire in his *dhoti* by wrapping a wet blanket (wetted with the same stolen water he had brought that morning) when he saw a *lathial* running away with a Gun in his hand. Forgetting the burn on his leg, Rudloo ran after the man. In his hand, the *lathial* still had the torch with which he set fire to Rudloo's hut and had attempted to roast him alive, and in the other hand he had the Gun. But at that time, Rudloo's eyes were focused only on the Gun. He could see nothing else.

He felt renewed strength in his legs—even the limping left leg.

The *lathial* turned back and saw Death pursuing him. If he stopped to take aim with his Gun, he would be overtaken by the vengeful Rudloo, and killed.

He stumbled over a thorny bush and fell headlong. The torch fell away from his hand and the Gun fell into the dust. He leapt to retrieve the Gun but at that moment, Rudloo also sprang like a tiger. The *lathial* got hold of the muzzle while Rudloo caught the wooden butt. Each tried to snatch it away from the other. In this tussle, Rudloo's finger happened to fall on the trigger and he pulled it.

There was a flash and an explosion and the *lathial* (who received the bullet in his chest) fell mortally wounded, or dead. There was no time to think, to speculate on the consequences. His own ominous fate was flickering before his eyes.

The police will come!

Rudloo will be arrested!

He will be tortured, then put before a court which would sentence him to death without going into the circumstances that had led to the accident and how the Gun had exploded in a scramble of life.

He will be hanged!

Suddenly, he realised that he had the Gun in his hand.

And in his ears rang the Comrade's words, "When the Gun falls into your hands, come over the hill beyond this village. There we live. There is *our* territory."

Who were "*We*"?

Other revolutionaries—like the Comrade who had defined revolution; *inquilab*—the great turning-over, when the sky will come down to the earth and the earth will go up to the sky!

They were waiting for him!

Comrade and his Comrades!!

Thinking this, he clutched the Gun firmly and started to run, despite the pain in his burnt left leg. He had to run across and over the hill.

While holding the heavy Gun in his hands, he suddenly felt its weight grow lighter,

like that walker with which he had learnt to walk,

like that little plough that Kaka Ram Deen had made for him, with which he used to play in his childhood,

like that *khurpee* with which he used to cut grass,

like that ink-soaked pen which he had thrown away one day and the ink had spread on the ground in the shape of a flower!

THE LAMP THAT BURNS ALL NIGHT

The clusters of graceful palms, reflected deep in the placid expanse of the backwaters, were silhouetted inky black against the sunset sky, aflame with clouds that were the colour of gold and fire—and blood!

A slow breeze caused gentle ripples in the otherwise mirror-like perfection of the inland sea. The distant melody of a fisherman's flute—now a clear, shrill bird-like note, now a mere whisper—seemed to enhance rather than shatter the all-pervading stillness.

My boatman, too, seemed caught by the mood of the evening and stopped paddling as the long, slim boat negotiated a curve around a triangular projection of land. It glided silently under the overhanging palms, breaking through the delicate filigreed pattern of their reflection in the water. Soon, we were out in the open again, but the boatman was silent, his oars lying idle by his side. The boat swayed gently with the ripples in the water, otherwise it was practically stationary. It was too peaceful, too beautiful, to be spoilt by any sound or movement. The boat, as well as the two men in it, was perfectly still. We were not going anywhere. Time itself seemed to have come to a stop.

I looked back. The town of Quilon, the white tops of its buildings barely visible above the palm-fringed coastline, was far, far away and the whisper of a train whistle came as if from another world. Here, where I was in a puny primitive boat, poised precariously on the gently heaving breast of the ocean, life was elemental, primeval. Here, the water was deep, very deep, the blue sky overhead was high, very high. The dark, little, semi-naked boatman night have been from another century, from another age altogether—when the earth was young and man had just learnt to build boats and light a fire by striking a flint stone!

The orange ball of the sun hesitated tremulously on the edge of the sea and then gracefully sank, leaving its rays for a brief moment to light up the western horizon and to touch the soft curves of the sea with burnished silver. But the glory of the sunset was short-lived and then, like a pall of death, darkness enveloped the earth and the sky.

I felt oppressed by the gloom and was about to suggest to the boatman to turn back to Quilon, back from that atmosphere and mood of ancient fantasy to civilisation and the present times, when something arrested my attention and the words I was about to utter froze on my lips. It was a pinpoint of light, moving in the distance like a ghost lantern gliding on the water. I was fascinated, intrigued and somewhat frightened by the curious phenomenon.

"What is that?" I asked the boatman, at last breaking the silence.

I thought it was odd that he did not look back as he replied with the merest suspicion of a tremor in his voice, "You shall soon see, Sahib."

A man of uncertain age, he spoke better English than one would expect from a boatman, even in Travancore, where I had found a surprisingly high percentage of literacy. It was, indeed, his fluency of speech and a certain intriguing—if not altogether engaging—gravity of expression which had prompted me to choose his rickety craft, rather than one of the noisy and crowded launches or the more dependable bigger boats which were lined up on the jetty. All through our leisurely cruise around the jigsaw puzzle of the backwaters, he had spoken very little and that had been a relief. For a more loquacious guide would have spoilt the peace of the evening by rattling off unnecessary information about the various landmarks we had passed. I was definitely not afflicted with the average tourist's craze for finding out and noting down names of every creek and island and lighthouse and picturesque hamlet that we passed on the way. I was out to savour the peace and beauty of these far-famed backwaters. And when I tired of the picture post card beauty of the landscape, I could look at the weather-beaten, leathery face of the boatman and speculate what kind of life he lived, what thoughts he thought, what emotions he felt, and what had caused those deeply-etched lines that gave his face a look of mocking gloom, as if he had seen through life and found it empty and without meaning.

"You shall soon see, Sahib," he had said and, without another word, had begun to paddle softly towards the light. After what appeared to be infinite suspense, the form of a boat detached itself from the darkness. There was someone—a woman, perhaps—in the boat and it was she who was holding a lantern in her hand.

Whither was she going at that dark hour, and why? Was she real or a figment of my imagination and conjured out of the darkness?

I noticed that the boatman took care not to draw too near the woman's boat but kept his distance, paddling very softly, almost inaudibly, so that we remained hidden in the dark. She did not see us, though I could now clearly see the outline of her slim figure in the circle of light that fell from her lantern. Her boat slowed down as it neared the top of a submerged stump of tree which, like some others I had seen that day, stood out of the water like a warning finger raised to the sky. Tied to this stump of tree was another lantern. The woman proceeded to fill it with kerosene oil and then struck a match to light it up.

As the lantern on that improvised lighthouse came to life, I could see her face. I still remember it vividly, for it was a face that one cannot easily forget. It provided a strange, inexplicable contrast between physical features and facial expression. It was pale, drawn, haggard, cheeks sunken into hollows, hair bedraggled. The hand with which she raised the wick of the lantern was thin and bony and bloodless. But in her big and undoubtedly beautiful eyes was an expression of infinite tenderness, a consecrated longing for something, for someone! And the face was lit up, as if by an inner flame that shone through that pale, almost transparent, skin of hers with selfless devotion. A smiling, happy face, and the light in her eyes was the light of hope. It was the kind of expression that you may expect to see on the face of a nun, or a saint—or a woman in love, waiting in hope for her love's return!

And so in this case she seemed to be, for as her boat turned around and went back in the direction of a little island where the outlines of some fishermen's huts could be seen dimly in the starlight, I heard her thin, reedy voice raised in a song—a plaintive, haunting melody, strange and yet familiar, which I seemed to have heard before and elsewhere, though not in that dialect of Malayalee boatmen.

"What is she singing?" I asked and the boatman replied, "It is a song of our people—the song that the woman sings while she waits for her man."

Ah, that was why she rowed up to that tree to light the lantern—so that her husband or lover should not lose his way in the dark! A touching scene but not by any means a strange phenomenon.

"And will he come tonight?" I asked, to make sure.

The boatman's voice, as it came to me out of the dark, was heavy with a strange weariness as he replied, not colloquially, in correct English; "No, sir, he will not come tonight or any night. He is dead. He has been dead for many years."

"And the woman?" I exclaimed, in utter surprise. "Doesn't she know that he is dead, that he will never come back?"

"She knows—maybe. But she will not believe. She still waits—and hopes..."

"...and every night, for many years, she comes and lights this lantern to guide the boat that will never come!" I spoke not to him but to myself as the significance of the strange human drama I had just seen enacted dawned upon me. My novelist's instinct was now thoroughly aroused and by unremitting questioning, I coaxed the whole story out, bit by bit, from the reticent boatman.

It was a story of the heroism of humble people. In 1942, when the revolutionary storm was raging all over the country, even the distant backwaters of Travancore became agitated. The prevalent but latent bitterness against the hated autocratic regime in the state found dramatic expression in a series of demonstrations on the part of students, workers and peasants. The boatmen of Quilon, several thousand strong, went on strike and, for two weeks, successfully resisted the coercion and persecution by the state police and were determined to stand by their demands "even if the backwaters became red with our blood".

"That's quite a picturesque, though grim, phrase," I commented as I listened to the simple-minded boatman. "Where did you hear it?"

"It was spoken by him, sir, in a meeting of the boatmen. Krishna, that was his name—a boatman and the son of a boatman. But he had been to school and lived in Trivandrum and had read many books and listened to the speeches of many leaders. He was a good, strong, young fellow and could swim the three miles from Quilon jetty to this island here to see his Radha..."

"Krishna and Radha! Isn't that too much of a romantic coincidence?"

My boatman was stumped by the word "coincidence" but when I explained that such things do not always happen in real life, he said, "Of course, sir, her name was not Radha but that is what he liked to call her. Radha and Krishna! Krishna and Radha! They were a good-looking pair and all the boatmen were glad they were going to be married..." Then he paused and corrected himself, "...that is, all except those who wanted Radha for themselves."

Then, unaccountably, he lapsed into silence and I had to provide a cue. "This Radha—she must have been very beautiful eight years ago?"

A sigh of recollection escaped his lips as he softly paddled the boat. "More than beautiful, sir. She was fairer than any other girl in these parts—tall and straight like a palm—and her skin was smooth and shiny like a fish, and her eyes! In her deep, black eyes was all the beauty of the backwaters."

We were moving away from the main story and getting bogged in poetic descriptions while I wanted the dramatic details. So I had to bring the conversation back into the proper channel with the usual, "And what happened then?"

"After that speech of his, there was a warrant for his arrest and the police were after him. They spread their net far and wide, but he went into hiding and was not caught. The police did not know but the boatmen and the fishermen did, that every night he swam through the dark waters to the island there to meet his Radha, and everyone laughed at the police and were happy at Krishna's daring, except those, who, as I said, who were jealous of him."

I had to puncture the silence again with my "what happened then?"

"Came the dark nights without the moon and a light appeared in the middle of the backwaters—just where you have seen it today—to guide the daring Krishna as he swam on his way to meet his girl. Night after night, as soon as it was dark, Radha would slip into a boat and row to this spot to light the lantern—just as she did today."

As I looked back at the lantern out there in the middle, I could almost hear the steady swish of water as the strong-armed Krishna negotiated the dark waters, guided by the life-saving pinpoint of light.

"And what happened then?"

From the depths of the boatman's soul, as it were, came his voice: "One night, the lantern was duly lit but it was blown out and there was no light to guide Krishna when he came swimming towards the island."

"What happened? Was there a storm?"

"You may say there was a storm, sir, but it was in the heart of an evil-minded man. He turned traitor to his people and caused the death of his friend by blowing out the lantern."

"But why? Why should a man do such a stupid, terrible thing?"

"He thought it was love—his love for Radha. The desire for her was strong in him—it was really like madness—and he knew he had no chance as long as Krishna was alive. He killed his friend as surely as if he had strangled him with his own hands. What he did not know was that he had no chance even after Krishna was dead."

We were now nearing the Quilon jetty and I was anxious to learn the end of the story and the rounding-up of all the principal characters.

"And so Krishna drowned. What happened then?"

"The strike was broken after Krishna's death."

"And Radha? How did she take her lover's death?"

"She did not believe he drowned. You see, the body was never found. So she still waits and lights that lantern every night for his return. They say she has gone mad."

"And that traitor, that fellow who caused Krishna's death, betrayed his people and the cause of their freedom? What happened to him?"

There was no reply from the boatman, who sat grimly, silent and hunched up; no reply except the steady, sigh-like swish of his oars. I could hear his guilty heartbeat, the water gently lapping against the sides of the boat, and the not-so-distant shrill whistle of the train that would take me away from Quilon, away from these enchanted backwaters, consecrated by the blood of the martyred Krishna and illuminated by Radha's little lantern which shone out of the surrounding gloom—a symbol of eternal hope!

THE NAKED FAKIR

(For Pankaj Kapoor)

No one knew where the fakir had come from.

No one knew to which religion he belonged.

Whoever asked received the same reply: "*Arrey baba*, I am a humble fakir. Do fakirs have names?"

Once, when the Municipal rationing authorities were checking ration cards, they approached him, holding the big register.

"What is your name?" one of them asked.

The old man replied, "Fakir."

"Your father's name?"

"Fakir."

"Where do you live?"

"Here, there, everywhere and nowhere."

One Municipal official winked at the other, tapping his forehead, "The poor fellow is obviously crazy."

Then they left. After that no one cared to interrogate the old man again.

No one had seen the fakir praying in the neighbourhood mosque.

No one had seen him performing *puja* in the temple just nearby.

Some Christians, full of hope, tried to take him to a church on Sunday, but that was in vain.

Some thought he was a follower of Sant Kabir.

Others thought he was another *Sai Baba* of Shirdi.

Still others imagined him to be a universal mendicant, a sadhu who had realised godhood and was, therefore, liberated from all denominational obligations.

All this was conjecture. But one fact was that everyone who came to him got his unsolicited blessings.

If a Hindu came, the fakir would say, "May *Bhagwan* fulfill all your desires."

If a Muslim came, he would say, "May Allah bless the good that you do."

If a Christian came, he would say, "May God bless your good deeds."

If by chance, an agnostic, a rationalist or an atheist came to him, he would say, "May Nature help you to help others."

The fakir, who was naked except for a brief loin cloth, had a patchwork quilt made of hundreds of pieces of red, green, yellow, blue, pink, black and white fabrics ranging from silk and nylon to the coarsest *khaddar*. It was old and dirty but large enough to serve all his needs.

During the day, he folded it and sat on it, cross-legged in meditation or in animated conversation with children going to or returning from school.

At night, he wrapped himself in it so that the quilt served both as a mattress and a blanket. But no one had ever seen him sleeping. Passers-by swore that he was awake at midnight, and at 4 a.m., when the milk van rattled to a stop, the fakir was still wide awake. Some people thought he suffered from chronic insomnia, while others felt, "When one has realised God, one doesn't need to sleep."

But the fakir reserved all his feelings for stray animals and the poor kids from the slums. This was natural since he was lying on the footpath near the biggest, dirtiest slum, Dharavi, where dozens of half-naked or completely naked children played in the gutters or huddled together under a tree to keep out of the rain. If he found anyone shivering, he would take the child into the warmth of his patchwork quilt, and all these children swore that though the quilt looked dirty from outside, when wrapped around, it emitted the fragrance of sandalwood *agarbatti*. When there were no children to snuggle up to him, he would give shelter to street dogs.

Once, the white-bearded and green-turbaned Imam Sahib of the mosque came up to him and said, "*Baba*, why don't you come to the mosque and pray?"

"What is the mosque?" asked the naked fakir, naively.

"The mosque," replied the Imam Sahib, "is the House of God."

"But God is here with me, in this quilt. Why should I search for him in the mosque?"

"*Laholwala quwwat!*" The Imam Sahib was provoked by the blasphemy, for he had seen unwashed children and dirty dogs emerging from under that quilt.

Some days later, the fakir was approached by the priest from the temple.

Folding his hands in a reverential salutation, the priest said, "*Namaste,* Maharaj."

The fakir retorted angrily, "Why do you abuse me?"

"Abuse?" The priest was genuinely surprised. "I just called you 'Maharaj'!"

"For a fakir to be called 'Maharaj' is an insult. Never say it again."

"All right, Baba, forgive me this time." The priest wondered at the man's idiosyncrasy but was determined to win him over. Indeed, he was determined to take him to the temple. The priest asked: "Why don't you come to the temple? At least come tomorrow."

"What is so special about tomorrow?" the fakir asked.

"It is Ram Naumi," informed the priest. "The birth of Lord Rama will be celebrated with a great *kirtan*."

"Your Rama may be born every year, but my Rama ever was and ever shall be. If you want to see Him, look inside this quilt!"

The priest was aghast. He returned to the temple, convinced that the fakir was not just naked but also demented.

Finally, the Christian padre arrived. He was pleased that the naked fakir had not agreed to go to the mosque or the temple.

"Holy Father," he addressed him, "You are the embodiment of the spirit of Christ. Your place is in our church."

"What is in your church?" asked the naked fakir.

"There are images of Lord Jesus Christ on the cross and of Mother Mary. There are pews for the congregation to sit on and kneelers to kneel upon. There are all comforts for true believers there."

The fakir asked, "Can I take my torn quilt there?"

The padre looked at the dirty quiet contemptuously: "What do you want this dirty quilt for? You won't need it. We will give you a new blanket. We will arrange a new bed with white sheets and pillows for you."

"But I can't discard my quilt. My whole life's earnings are in it. I can't go anywhere without it."

At that moment, a dirty dog emerged from its folds and started barking at the padre.

"Eh, Kaloo!" the fakir reprimanded the dog, "This is Padre Sahib. A very big and holy man, you impertinent one!" Then, turning to the padre, he said, "It is a dumb animal, you know."

The padre, however, concluded that this was really the devil with his dog, Cerberus. Without a word he took to his heels, making the sign of the cross to ward off evil spirits.

The padre mentioned the incident in his Sunday sermon and said that the naked Hindu fakir claimed he had wealth hidden in the dirty old quilt. Michael, who had come to the church to steal silver candlesticks, heard about this and promptly hurried off to his Hindu friend and colleague, Ramu. He said he had heard it from no less reliable a source than the padre of the church, that there were thousands of rupees hidden inside the dirty old quilt of the naked fakir. Ramu repeated the story with a bit of embellishment to his Muslim friend, Masita. "The naked fakir, whom I always suspected to be a fraud, has thousands of gold sovereigns hidden in his dirty old quilt."

An unwritten pact was "signed" between the three. They already knew each other. Picking pockets was their main occupation. Sometimes they used a big, sharp knife to threaten lonely people at night to part with their possessions. Sometimes they even played the chilli powder trick to get what they wanted.

One day, they had pinched a man's wallet but when they gathered at their *jhopadpatti*, they found in it only a Second-Class railway pass, a laundry receipt, a photograph of a plain-looking, young girl and two rupees and forty paisa.

"We won't get more than eighty paisa each," said Ramu, dismally.

Masita said, "Then what are we to do?"

"What I told you earlier," said Michael, "Let us relieve the naked fakir of his gold sovereigns. The padre himself had said the bugger has lakhs sewn up in that wretched quilt of his."

"Then let us do it immediately. I haven't had a square meal the whole week," Ramu complained.

"When we divide the gold," said Michael, "you can have hundred bloody square meals."

Masita added, "You and your meals! I will do something better. That mutton-seller wants ₹2,000 for his stepdaughter, Samina."

Ramu added, "I will open a shop and sell vegetables. Do you know what the price of onions is today? Twelve rupees a kilo!"

"To hell with your onions," Michael exploded, "I haven't paid the greengrocer a paisa even once. I will bring them *free* from your shop, too."

"*Abey saley,*" warned Ramu, abusively, "If you so much as touch my onions, I will break your hands."

"Go on and try it!" retorted Michael, "Let's see your guts, you son of a *bania*!"

There would have been a violent tussle between them if Masita hadn't intervened: "You mad fellows, you have already started quarrelling. Let us first pinch the quilt, at least. That bastard sleeps on it, and then there are those cursed dogs. If they wake up, they will bark their heads off and make all the people from the *jhopadpatti* gather."

"Don't worry about them," assured Michael, "If they make any sound, I'll beat them to death."

"No need to beat them. It will create a racket. If even one of them escapes, he will howl and attract a crowd. I have a better plan."

"What is it?" asked Michael.

"I will get some pieces of meat and bones from Bundu the butcher and, by smearing a lot of rat poison on them, we will first finish off the dogs quietly,"

"That," conceded Michael, "is a sensible plan."

"Then we will finish off the naked fakir, too," said Ramu. "One stroke of my iron rod will crack the bugger's skull."

"That's right. You bring your iron rod with you," said Michael. "It's a mighty useful thing. I will bring my knife, and Masita, you bring that iron *danda* of yours."

So that night, after the midnight police patrol had passed, the three armed crooks approached the place where the naked fakir was sleeping—or feigning sleep. Masita held the paper packet containing the poisoned meat.

They found the fakir bundled up in his quilt, so they were not sure whether he was awake or asleep.

Masita first placed the poisoned meat on the ground near the quilt. One by one, three dogs emerged—of which one was a mere puppy. The three crooks hid behind a tree.

Masita wondered how any human being could endure the company of these dirty, unclean, diseased animals, under the same cover.

The dogs went straight to the meat pieces. First, the two bigger dogs licked the pieces, then bit into them. Their strong jaws closed in on the bones with a crushing sound. The puppy was content to lick the pieces with his little pink tongue and was the first to whimper and fall down—dead! The bigger dogs took longer to succumb to the pangs of death. The three "murderers" feared the whimpering of the dogs would awaken the naked fakir. But he slept soundly.

When they were sure that the dogs were finally dead, the three *goonda*s picked up enough courage to come out of the shadows.

Slowly, stealthily, they tip-toed to the fakir. Michael tentatively tried to lift a corner of the quilt, but found it too heavy.

"It's heavy," he whispered to his companions.

"That means," whispered Ramu, "there is a lot of wealth hidden in it." And he thought gleefully, "My share will be enough to open my shop. With black-marketing in vegetables and a bit of smuggling, I will be all set for life."

Masita also touched the corner of the quilt and found it heavy as if it was loaded with silver or gold. He dreamt of the mutton-seller's stepdaughter, whom he would acquire for ₹2,000.

Michael, with his iron rod, stood where he thought the fakir's head was.

Masita positioned himself in the middle, knife in hand, its blade shining in the moonlight.

Ramu stood at the other end and was certain that with one stroke of the stout stick, he would break the fakir's legs.

Michael was their leader in this operation. He commanded in a whisper.

"One."

"Two."

"Three."

The three lethal weapons fell simultaneously on the body of the naked fakir. There was the sound of a skull bone cracking as the knife slashed through the quilt and sank into the body.

Then all three of them placed their hands on the quilt and pulled at it simultaneously.

But underneath, there was no fakir, naked or otherwise!

There was nothing at all under the quilt.

The three looked at each other with awe and wonderment.

Michael snatched the quilt from the hands of his companions and fled.

Ramu and Masita chased him.

Michael ran towards the marshy beach. There, in the sea, lay his boat. He was sure that once he got there, nobody would be able to catch him. He knew a dozen secret places where he could hide for days.

But Ramu was also agile and, at that moment, spurred on by greed and anger. Michael was slowed down by the reeds and slush of the marshy land. Ramu and Masita caught up with him and they all tried to snatch the dirty quilt away from each other. They tugged and pulled and violently jerked it about till it tore into bits. But nothing came out of it, expect the old, dirty, odorous cotton with which it was stuffed. All three of them pounced on the rags, hoping to find a fortune, but they got nothing.

Michael was the first to realise the futility of their search. In anger, he exclaimed: "This fakir was a bloody fraud, I tell you."

"Not a fakir," corrected Ramu, "He was a *goonda*!"

"Not just an ordinary *goonda,* but one who could perform magic," added Masita. "Didn't you see how he dissolved into nothingness when we pounced to kill him?"

Ever since that day, Masita, Ramu and Michael gave up their life of crime.

Michael became a mechanic, Ramu an assistant in a grocer's shop, and Masita got a job at the docks as a loader.

It was hard work, but they enjoyed it.

Later they heard that in the Bandra *jhopadpatti*, a mysterious naked fakir was seen, with a patchwork quilt in which he let slum children and stray dogs sleep with him.

But Masita, Ramu and Michael couldn't find the time to go and see for themselves whether it was the same naked fakir, even though they had also heard that there was a fortune hidden in the patchwork quilt.

FATHERS AND SONS

"...immortal sons defying their fathers..."

—Plato

"All right, just as you please! You will never see my face again."

"You will never see my face again!"

"Never! Never!! Never!!!"

Like an unending refrain, the words were still ringing in the ears of Thakur Krishen Singh. Their lingering echo was mocking, annoying and insulting him. For the first time in his life, he felt paralysed with rage, powerless to do anything, dazed with the impact of the incredible situation. It was unbelievable but true that he, Thakur Krishen Singh, before whom the sturdiest peasant trembled with fear, had been defied—and defeated—by his own son.

"My son!" he mused bitterly, "my own son!"

How could he disobey and defy his father! How dare he leave the house where he was born, the homestead of his ancestors! How dare he!

And yet he had dared and he was gone...gone forever. Forever! That's what he had said. There was finality in those words—for ever! There was an ominous ring of finality also in the receding clatter of his unpolished, down-at-heel shoes as he walked away, for the last time, through the marble-floored corridor. There was finality in those measured footsteps, finality and a grim determination, a challenge and a declaration of war, as if they, too, were proclaiming: "I will never come back. Never! Never!! Never!!!"

Twirling his grey but stiffly curled-up moustaches, a mechanical reflex action of which he was hardly conscious, he thought to himself, "What is the world coming to? The peasants are defying the landlords, sons are disobeying their fathers and leaving their homes. Centuries-old bonds are breaking, hallowed social traditions and institutions are being trampled into dust. Not only has the country been partitioned, but every home, every family, is being rent in twain. Sons are leaving their fathers, daughters are getting alienated from their mothers, husbands and wives are being divorced. There is disunity and disruption in the oldest joint families. Why? Why?? Why???"

The question came crashing through his mind.

Why, oh, why?

He put his question to the walls of his luxurious drawing room, to the portraits of his ancestors, whose lifeless eyes were glaring at him; to the ivory statuettes of Bhagwan Shree Krishna, and his beloved Radha, who seemed so serenely indifferent to the worries and woes of man; to the marble bust of the Buddha and the bronze bust of Mahatma Gandhi, who were peacefully smiling from their pedestals; to the khaddar tri-colour which adorned the wall; to Bharat Mata in a gilded frame; to the tall, carved stone pillars which supported the high roof; to the leather-bound law books in glass shelves; to the wall calendar which was fluttering in the breeze like the "bird of time"; to the ornamental clock on the mantelpiece which was ticking out some strange but beautiful message; to the steel safe in the corner which contained jewels and notes and property deeds worth at least a million.

And, finally, he put this question to his snow-white, starched Gandhi cap which was placed, as usual, on the top of the safe—like a crown on a throne!

Why all this discontent, this confusion, this disobedience, this lack of faith? Why this storm in the placid waters of society which had remained undisturbed for a thousand years? Why?

Why?

From his silent lips, this question went bouncing round the room like a rubber ball, ricocheting from the frescoed ceiling to the portraits on the wall, from the wall to the marble floor, bouncing back to the ceiling, over and over again. But there was no answer. Walls, pictures, statues—all were silent. Silent and, perhaps, astonished like him. Not only the drawing room, but the whole vast mansion seemed empty, deserted, forlorn. As if his son, his rude, impertinent, disobedient, rebellious son had taken away with him the very soul of the house! Or, maybe, he was the life and soul of the house. And, now that he was gone, this vast and luxuriously furnished house was dead—like the tombs of the pharaohs in which every conceivable convenience and comfort and ornament was buried. Everything—except life!

Anand—his son!

Twenty-five years ago, he had named his first-born Anand—for he had, indeed, brought both happiness and success in his life. The day he was born, Krishen Singh had won his first case in the District Court. There had been much talk of it in legal circles and since then, many important cases had come his way. But to Krishen Singh, that first big case had been a source of real joy—for he had saved from the gallows an innocent but unfortunate man who, by a conspiracy of circumstances, had got wrongly involved in a murder charge. He had received a very small fee from the poor client, but the gleam of gratitude that Krishen Singh saw in that simple peasant's eyes had been reward enough for all his labours. Justice and Humanity—these were the ideals to which the young lawyer had decided to dedicate his life.

Justice, Humanity and Freedom! When Krishen Singh heard this slogan uttered by a veteran Congress leader, he felt that it was an echo of his heart-beats, the strident call of his hot, youthful blood.

Anand was four years old when his father went on his first "pilgrimage" to prison: Krishen Singh was sentenced to three years Rigorous Imprisonment (RI) for a "seditious speech"—a mockery of the same law that he had sought to serve in the courts! He had mused on the irony of it during the years that he spent in jail. An unknown young lawyer was not given the consideration and comforts that were vouchsafed some of the elder leaders. To be herded in a barrack, along with common criminals, was no picnic. But Krishen Singh bore the rigours of prison life with characteristic Rajput fortitude. The separation from his wife and child was a torture, indeed, but he knew many thousands of patriots were suffering likewise. He had at least the consolation that his family was not suffering from want, as they had lands and property and his father was there to look after the daughter-in-law and grandson—even if he did not agree with the politics of his son!

Then, one day, a few months before he was due to be released, he received a letter written in a shaky, childish hand. "My dear Pitaji—namaste". And, vaulting over the stone walls, the sweet memories of his son came to illuminate his dark and dingy cell. His son, whose face was a reproduction of his own features, was the living symbol of his love for Radha! In the childish scrawl and ink-stains, he could see the beloved innocent face smiling at him, beckoning him, complaining of such a long absence from home. For a few moments, Krishen Singh's very ideals seemed to falter as the yearning for his son and wife came surging into his heart. He felt like breaking the iron bars and rushing home straight. But the next moment, as he read through the letter, he felt ashamed of the momentary weakness of his spirit. For his son had written: "Pitaji, you don't worry about Mataji. I am here to see she is ollrite: Mataji she say when i becum big i also shud becum rewolooshanari like you, Pitaji."

A couple of weeks later, he learnt that his wife was ill. Anand wrote: "Mataji she become very thin and weak and remember you all time."

Some friends advised him to apply for parole on the grounds of his wife's illness, but Radha herself wrote a letter with her own trembling hand: "Please do not compromise your ideals on my account; otherwise I will never forgive myself. I don't want you to beg for a favour from this government. If I am lucky, I will have your darshan when you are released in due course."

Krishen Singh tore up the application for parole. Then the Gandhi-Irwin truce was signed and Krishen Singh, along with other satyagrahis, was released. When he reached his town, he was taken around in a procession. But when he reached home, there was no Radha to greet him at the door. Only Anand, grown taller and thinner in three years, stood there alone. Not a flicker of a smile appeared in his face when he saw his father—he just looked up with his eyes brimful with tears. Then, mustering up his sobs, he spoke. "Pitaji, you have come too late. Mataji is gone."

Since then, father and son had been left to themselves. Every evening, on returning from court, Krishen Singh would lie down on an easy chair and ask his son: "Well, Anand, how did it go at school today?" Anand would tell him everything: "Today I fell down from the jamun tree, see I got this injury on my shin... Today the English Army soldiers were going on a march on the road in front of our school. All red-faced like monkeys. They were angrily looking at us as if they would eat us. Many boys got frightened and ran away but I was not afraid."

And Krishen Singh would say, "Shabash, son, well done! That's what I expected from you."

When Anand was 10 years old, one day he had come back from school and said: "Pitaji, they have turned me out of school. Because I wear a Gandhi cap, the Headmaster had already warned me. Today some English Inspector came to our school—his face was red but became redder when he saw my Gandhi cap—and of all the boys he asked me to give a list of the blessings of the British Raj. What could I do, Pitaji? I had to say that the government kept my father and many great leaders like Gandhiji in jail—what bigger blessing could there be? At this he was furious and caned me six times on each hand—see, Pitaji, here are the marks. But I did not cry before that Englishman, Pitaji, I did not cry..." And saying this, he had buried his face in the lap of his father and burst into tears. And Krishen Singh, proud of his son, had tenderly lifted his face, and kissed him.

Today, 15 years later, Krishen Singh could still feel his cheek wet with those hot tears of his son.

Having sent Anand to Benaras to study, Krishen Singh was left alone in the house, devoting most of his time to court work and only occasionally finding time for local Congress politics. Soon, he had a roaring practice. His income rose from hundreds to thousands, for now he did not ask a client whether he was innocent or guilty, he only wanted to know if he could afford his fee.

In every way, Krishen Singh was progressing and prospering—from District Court to High Court, from membership to presidentship of the Municipality, from District Congress Committee to the Provincial Congress Committee. Already there was talk that in the coming elections to the Provincial Assembly, he would be put up as a Congress candidate. He thought: "Anand should be pleased with all this when he comes home for the holidays."

When the son came back from college, Krishen Singh was satisfied to see that books comprised the bulk of his luggage which meant that, he was not wasting time in loafing and gadding about, like other boys. But most of these were not textbooks but collections of poems in Hindi and English and works on the French, Irish, American and

Russian revolutions. "I am so glad you are also interested in politics," commented Krishen Singh. "I am sure, like your father, you will also become a politician."

"I am sorry, Pitaji," Anand had replied, "But I don't want to become a politician—I want to be a revolutionary."

And Krishen Singh, with a half-hearted chuckle, had said: "Of course, of course, we all want to bring about a revolution." But he was dismayed to find that from the expression on his son's face, he did not believe it.

Anand had been home for a few days when am old peasant came with a complaint. The zamindar, he said, had turned him out of his holding and the zamindar's toughs had beaten him and his sons and burnt his hut. He pleaded and whined and begged Krishen Singh to take up his case. "Vakil Saab," he implored, "please get me back my land. I will forever pray for you and your children." But Krishen Singh's clerk demanded to know if he could afford the fee of such a great lawyer. The peasant, with trembling hands, untied a knot in his loincloth and produced a dirty, crumpled, five-rupee note. The clerk was pushing the old man when Anand happened to enter the house. Years had passed since then but Krishen Singh still remembered that conversation—as if it was the first act of the drama that had reached the climax today.

"Why, Pitaji, why are you not taking up this poor old man's case?"

The clerk tried to intervene with his oily tongue: "Chhotay Thakur, you don't know these fellows, these rogues, they don't have a pie and they come just to harass us..."

"I want to hear Pitaji's reply."

"Munshiji is right, son."

"Then you take up his case. I will give you whatever fee you demand."

For a few moments, Krishen Singh was stunned into silence. Then he said: "After all, we have our lands, too. Today if I take up this case, tomorrow my own tenants may turn against me. Already they are growing uppish and rude. Tomorrow they may try to dispose us, the landlords!"

"That, of course, is bound to happen when landlordism is abolished."

"You are talking like a fool."

"I am not talking like a fool, Pitaji. I am talking like you—as you once used to do!"

The next day, Anand said: "I have to prepare for the examination. I want to go back to Benaras and study there during the rest of the holidays." And the father, nursing his hurt pride, did not even once ask him to stay on.

From that day onwards, the gulf between the thoughts and feelings of father and son continued to widen. During the holidays, when Anand came home and they happened to have a discussion on something, Krishen Singh felt that he was talking not to his son but to a complete stranger.

Thakur Krishen Singh was elected to the Assembly on a Congress ticket and received congratulations from thousands—but not from his son! Anand won the first prize in the All-India Debating Competition, but that gave no pleasure to his father, for the subject of the debate was "The Salvation of India Lies In Socialism Alone", and Anand had made a fiery speech in support of it.

Thakur Krishen Singh presided over the Zamindar Conference. Anand joined the Congress Socialist Party.

Thakur Krishen Singh inaugurated the Rajput Yuvak Sabha. Anand founded the Marxist Study Circle.

Thakur Krishen Singh went to England to plead a taluqdar's inheritance case in the Privy Council and received a fee of over a lakh rupees. About the same time, Anand was expelled from the University for his connection to the revolutionary movement. When the war started, Thakur Krishen Singh, along with other chosen satyagrahis, duly informed the Superintendent of Police that they would perform satyagraha at a specified time and place, and the superintendent very politely arrested him and conveyed him in his own car to jail where he was given A–class treatment. Released after three months, Thakur Krishen Singh decided not to court imprisonment again, but to do the "constructive" work of propagating khadi. But secretly, he took a government contract (in a friend's name) to supply boots to the Army which yielded him a profit of a couple of lakhs in a year.

Anand took out a procession against India's forced participation in the war and, after receiving several blows in the lathi charge, he was kicked by a tommy with an iron-shod boot—perhaps one of the very boots that his father had supplied!

On August 9, 1942, Thakur Krishen Singh, alone with other prominent leaders, was taken in a special train and made a "royal guest" in an old but comfortable fort. On the same day, Anand received lathi blows, was almost choked by tear gas, and was arrested for trying to hoist the national flag.

During his detention, Thakur Krishen Singh made a reverent study of the Bhagavad Gita and the philosophy of yoga. During his detention, Anand studied Marx's Capital and other Marxist literature.

The government allowed Thakur Krishen Singh to get his cook to prepare his favourite dishes, just as he used to make them in the Thakur Sahib's own kitchen. Anand, along with other C-class political prisoners in his jail, went on a hunger strike for 17 days.

During his term of detention, thanks to his regular life and enforced rest, Thakur Krishen Singh's weight increased by 10 pounds. During the same period, due to the hunger strike, Anand's weight decreased by 15 pounds.

And then Anand escaped from prison and went "underground", secretly working in the revolutionary movement. Once, the police got scent of him and almost captured him, but he gave them the slip—with a bullet wound in his leg.

The wound could not be attended to for several days and got septic. For two months, Anand lay sick in a friend's house. It was while he was still unable to walk about that he read his father's statement in the papers, in the course of which he had said: "I strongly condemn my son's terroristic activities."

Then the negotiations between the Congress and the government resumed and Thakur Krishen Singh was released along with other leaders. After a few months, when the warrant against him was cancelled, Anand came home to see his father and to rest for some time before resuming his political work. Krishen Singh was shocked and dismayed to see that his son had been reduced to a mere skeleton. For the time being, he forgot all their political differences and, as he embraced Anand, there were tears in the eyes of both father and son.

June 3, 1947, brought with it the Mountbatten Award.

India was partitioned—even as she became free, communal passions flared up, and the minorities began to be massacred in Pakistan and in parts of India. Anand threw himself into the task of stemming the tide of hatred and violence and saving the lives and honour of his Muslim comrades. Saleem, his friend and co-worker from his "Quit India" days, was in imminent danger in his village in Bihar when Anand rushed there and brought him and his family to the safety of his home. He was certain that, being a Congressman, his father would welcome these nationalist Muslims who had always opposed and consequently suffered at the hands of the fanatical elements in their own community.

But Krishen Singh said to his son: "Better put up your Muslim friends somewhere else. People are beginning to point their fingers at us and saying that we have given refuge to Muslims."

Anand replied: "But they are not merely Muslims, they are nationalists. They have always been with the Congress and against the Muslim League."

"Maybe you are right. But do you not know what is happening in Pakistan?"

"The same that is happening here, that is happening in your heart," Anand retorted. And that very night he left his home and went away elsewhere, with his friend and his family.

Like images on a cinema screen, these events continued to flash across Krishen Singh's memory.

His friends would say: "Thakur Sahib, you have given too much latitude to your son. He is becoming a rebel in every way." And he would reply: "Don't worry. He is young still. In youth, all of us dream of becoming rebels and revolutionaries. I was like that myself. He was sure that in the course of time the hot-blooded youth would cool down, both physically and psychologically, and come back home.

But Anand did not come back. When he did come, it was not as an affectionate son but as an agent of the "enemy".

Thakur Krishen Singh had kept himself aloof from the wrangle for ministership. He had also virtually retired from the Provincial Congress Committee. He was again concentrating on his practice and making a few thousand every month. But, after the establishment of the national government, he believed it was the duty of every patriot to give a fillip to Indian industries. Of course, he had not overlooked the fact that it was particularly desirable in his case to do so, because of the imminent abolition of zamindari...though there would be compensation enough to invest in industry! And so he and some of his friends had bought a couple of mills in Cawnpore (Kanpur) from a British firm that was quitting India. Due to his influence, it was easy to get government contracts and other facilities. And thus Thakur Krishen Singh, Advocate, became Seth Krishen Singh, Mill-owner!

But unfortunately, the path of national progress in industry was blocked by Socialist and Communist boulders. The workers were on strike. The mills were closed and no smoke came out of the chimneys.

Krishen Singh's manager, with many years of experience of strike-breaking, advised that some way be found to disrupt the workers' unity. The "loyal" workers must be tempted with extra wages, the picketers should be terrorised by hired hoodlums and the government should be persuaded to arrest the trade union leaders as disturbers of peace. But Seth Krishen Singh, who was still an amateur in the ways of capitalism, advised against any such means being adopted. He wanted to first try his legal acumen in an argument with the trade unionists. So he asked his manager to inform the strikers that he would like to talk things over with their leader.

Seth Krishen Singh was shocked to see the leader of the strikers. It was Anand. His son! He had changed a great deal in the last few months. He was unshaven; his clothes were shabby; his eyes were sunken with fatigue, but there was a bright new gleam in them. Also there was a tough timbre in his voice. Today he had come to bargain on behalf of the "enemy". But still, he was his son. The father's heart missed a beat with a sudden surge of emotion.

"I have not come to ask for a bribe," Anand had said in greeting. "You are my father. So, as a son, I have come to warn you of the danger you are in."

"Danger?"

"Yes—imminent danger."

Krishen Singh thought that the workers were, perhaps, conspiring to murder him, and Anand had come to warn him. But Anand soon disabused him.

"No, no there is no danger to your life. The danger against which I am warning you is to your society, to your economic system, to your government."

The old discussion of Capitalism and Socialism was once again resumed, but this time Krishen Singh used a new weapon of attack: "Anand, have you ever considered that this mill which you and your strikers are out to destroy is soon to be your property?" And then, coughing to proclaim asthma: "I don't expect to last very long, you know."

Anand had countered with a smile. "But your social system is not going to last very long, either. Capitalism is already dead. Don't try to tempt me with a piece of flesh from this stinking corpse."

That provoked the pent-up anger of the father. "Remember, Anand, I will disinherit you, you will not get a single pie..."

"Don't worry Pitaji, I have already disowned your property and your society."

Once again, controlling his temper, Krishen Singh tried to reason with his son. "Listen to me, Anand. Leave this nonsense of Communism and Socialism. After all, I am your father and what I want is only for you own good. Isn't it your duty to do as I say?"

"Did you always act according to the wishes of your father, Pitaji?" Anand put a counter question and went on, "it would be horribly unnatural if sons began obeying their fathers. Do you know if sons—'immortal sons', Plato called them—had not defied their fathers, we would still be living in caves and dressing in skins, lighting fires by rubbing stones, believing the earth to be flat, and worshipping the sun and snakes and trees!" Then, smiling in his characteristic manner, he concluded: "Pitaji, believe me, the secret of progress lies in sons disagreeing with and disobeying their fathers."

Krishen Singh was not willing to enter into a philosophical discussion. He was only concerned with the loss he was suffering because of the strike and it was a shocking thing that his own son should be responsible for it.

Gradually, his tone became harsher. "Do you know it is only because of me that you have not yet been arrested in connection with the strike? I did not want that rough methods should be used to bring the workers to their senses. I would have been glad if the whole unpleasant affair could be amicably settled. But now I will be forced to..."

"To have a warrant issued for my arrest?" Anand completed the sentence. "Soon you will be forced to have us lathi charged and fired at. You have no idea how many atrocities Capitalism will force you to commit."

Could this rude, impertinent, wild-eyed and ill-mannered agitator be his son? No. No! He couldn't be!

"Get out of here," Krishen Singh screamed. "From today I am not your father and you are not my son. I don't want to have anything to do with you."

"That I knew long ago, on the very day you refused to take up the case of that poor peasant, and again on the day you issued that statement against me to placate the government and when you refused protection to my friends because they were Muslims."

"Get out! I don't want to see your face or hear your voice." Krishen Singh's mighty voice went booming up to the ceiling.

Anand's voice, by contrast, was low-pitched; but his tone was deliberate and sharp, like a razor. "All right, just as you please! You will never see my face again."

Then he had gone and there was an ominous ring of finality in the receding clatter of his polished, down-at-heel shoes as he walked away—for the last time—through the marble-floored corridor. There was grim determination in those measured footsteps, a challenge and a declaration of war. "I will never come back. Never! Never!! Never!!!

The house was grimly desolate—and so was the heart of Krishen Singh! Everything in the room—every wall, every portrait, every statue—mocked at him. Within him, he knew that it was not an enemy whom he had turned out of the house but his only son—a curly-haired child who had once written to his father, "I also shud become rewolooshanari like you," an eager, bright-eyed boy who had shown the cane mark on his hands and said, "But I did not cry before that Englishman, Pitaji, I did not..." and had thenm burst into tears! Today he had turned out not only his son, but also the mother of his son, his wife Radha, who had written to him in prison: "If I am lucky, I will have your darshan when you are released", who had died but not allowed her husband to compromise his principles by seeking a favour from the government.

Having turned out his son, he was alone in the whole world. But no, he had at least one relation—his aged father, Thakur Harnam Singh, who lived alone in their old family house in the village. The old man, now nearly 70, was in his dotage and, perhaps, not quite in his senses. Krishen Singh rarely saw him. But he would go to him and tell him how he felt about Anand. Only a father would be able to understand what Krishen Singh was feeling today.

He ordered the car from the garage and was soon on the dusty road to the village.

The old Thakur was busy with his evening puja when Krishen Singh's car reached there. Disturbed in his moments of devotion by the electric horn, he bawled out at the servants: "You idiots! Haven't I told you a thousand times that I want no chariot of the rakshasas to enter my compound? Do you want me to turn it to ashes right now with a curse?"

Thakur Harnam Singh had a booming voice that could be heard from half a mile away. He was near-blind, but would not agree to using foreign glasses; he was toothless but would not allow a dentist to make a set of false teeth for him. Krishen Singh went in and stood right in front of his father but still the old man failed to recognise him.

"Who is that?"

"It's me—Krishen."

"Begone, you imposter! Krishna Bhagwan would never come in a chariot of the rakshasa." Saying this, he began to count his holy beads while intoning the names of God.

"Pitaji, I am not Krishna Maharaj, I am your son—Krishen."

"I have no son. Nor am I anyone's father."

Many years ago, when Krishen Singh had joined the non-cooperation movement, Thakur Harnam Singh had uttered these words while turning his son out of the house. Now, in his dotage, he had lost his memory and all sense of time and place; in his mind Bhagwan Krishna and Krishen Singh, the past and the present, had become hopelessly and inextricably mixed up.

"Pitaji, please listen to me. I am your son, Krishen Singh. I want to tell you something. My son Anand has left home forever."

"Yes, yes," the old man assented, his mind still wandering in the past, "Krishen has left home. I have myself turned him out."

"He has become a Socialist—he is leading a strike in my own mill," Krishen Singh tried desperately to explain matters to his father and to get his sympathy.

"Yes, I know, I know, it is all due to that man Gandhi. It is he who is inciting and corrupting the young men. Collector Sahib has told me that."

"I am talking of Anand, Pitaji," Krishen Singh shouted. The old man's mental wanderings into the past were getting on his nerves.

"I assure you, Collector Sahib, I will threaten to turn him out of the house and he will come to his senses. The Thakurs have been loyal to His Majesty for seven generations. How can a son of the Thakurs join these rebels?"

Once again, Krishen Singh tried to put sense into the head of the old man. "Pitaji, please understand, this is not 1922, it is 1950. Your grandson has left home to join the Socialists. He wants to finish us all—landlords and aristocrats and businessmen."

But the old man continued to mutter words that were echoes from the past. "The king is the incarnation of God. Whoever revolts against the king will be damned in this world and the next."

Krishen Singh was pining for just one word of sympathy from his father to console him in this hour of desolation. "Pitaji," he pleaded in a desperate tone, "is it not shameful that he has turned an enemy of his own class, his own family, of his own father—the father who fed him and clothed him and brought him up with so much love and care?"

"It is a terrible thing," the old Thakur shouted and Krishen Singh felt that for once sense had penetrated his father's fossilised brain. But the next moment he was disillusioned, for Harnam Singh was saying: "It is a terrible thing, indeed. The angrezi sarkar is our father and our mother; but for the sarkar we zamindars would have been nobodies—how can one of our sons turn against the sarkar? No, no, it can never be."

Now, Krishen Singh remembered that many, many years ago, his father had said these words to him when he had joined the Congress. Some trick of fate had set the old record on the gramophone of memory.

"Pitaji, what are you talking about? This is 1950. We are free now. The angrezi sarkar has willingly given us our freedom. Today the position is quite different. This Anand and his friends, these Socialists and Communists..."

"This is all the mischief of that Gandhi. Today he is inciting the people against the government, tomorrow he will incite the peasants against the landlords. This fire of revolt, once lighted, will not be easy to put out..."

"Pitaji, they are setting the country on fire with their talk of class wars..."

"They want freedom," the toothless old man said mockingly, "they shout 'Inqilab Zindabad!' Even the son of Thakur Sangram Singh has joined these hooligans..."

"Pitaji!" Krishen Singh cried. He felt he would go mad if his father continued to ramble about the past.

"Remember, son," the old man's voice boomed shakily but powerfully, "I will disinherit you. You will not get a single pie..."

Who had uttered these words? When? Had his father said that to him 25 years ago, or had he himself said that to Anand a few hours earlier? Krishen Singh's mind was in a confused whirl. The past and the present were getting hopelessly mixed in his memory, too.

Tears were glistening in the myopic eyes of the old Thakur as he spoke in a voice that was trembling with emotion: "Listen to me, son. Leave this nonsense of Gandhi and Congress. After all, I am your father and what I want is only for your own good. Isn't it your duty to do as I say?"

"It would be horribly unnatural if sons began obeying their fathers. Do you know if sons had not defied their fathers, we would still be living in caves and dressing in skins, lighting fires by rubbing stones, believing the earth to be flat, and worshipping the sun and snakes and trees! Pitaji, believe me, the secret of progress lies in sons disagreeing with and disobeying their fathers."

Krishen Singh was astonished to hear these words uttered by his own tongue.

His father was shouting: "Get out! I don't want to see your face or hear your voice."

"All right, just as you please. You will never see my face again," he said, but he had a strange feeling that he had seen this drama and heard this dialogue, somewhere before. Was he also losing his mind?

Leaving his father alone, he came away.

When he returned to his own house, the drawing room was brilliantly lit up and all the doors were open as if waiting for someone's arrival. Everything was as he had left it. His ancestors stared at him from their framed portraits on the walls—Krishan Bhagwan and his beloved Radha were lost in their immortal, ethereal love. There was a smile of understanding in marble face of the Buddha and an amused smile on the bronze face of Mahatma

Gandhi. The snow-white starched Gandhi cap still lay on the top of the safe. Everything was silent, motionless, dead! Except the wall calendar which was fluttering in the breeze like the bird of time, and the old clock which was tick-ticking some strange and significant message.

One by one, Krishen Singh put out the lights, and the palatial luxurious house that was like a Pharoah's tomb was now shrouded in eternal darkness.

FIVE FACES OF MOTHER INDIA

To the German, his country is Fatherland, the American symbolises the United States as "Uncle Sam", the Britons like to imagine themselves as children of the strong, masculine, whiskered John Bull, and the Frenchman is devoted to his La Patrie. For the people of India, however, since time immemorial, the country is Bharat Mata, Bharat, the Mother, or Mother India!

Vande Mataram (Glory to the Mother)! *Bharat Mata Ki Jai* (Glory to Mother India)! The most popular slogans of the Indian national movement, which Mahatma Gandhi led, refer to the country as "Mother"! It may be a psychological throwback to the ancient matriarchal traditions of our country or just a poetic symbolism based on the life-giving attributes of motherhood. To the Indian, if his country is Bharat Mata or Mother India, the earth itself is Dharti Mata or Mother Earth!

The concept of a collective Mother India is, no doubt, perfectly logical. But it is only through an individual that we can evoke the emotional imagery of the country as mother. Each of us will symbolise Bharat Mata in a different form, inevitably a feminine one—some saw her incarnated in the versatile genius of Sarojini Naidu, others in the selfless humility of Kasturba. Personally, whenever I have thought of personalising Mother India, I have thought of five humble, unknown women who, between them, summed up and symbolised the eternal grace, the life-giving maternal devotion, the earthy wisdom and abiding faith that one likes to associate with the concept of Supreme Mother.

1. KHADDAR SHROUD

The first of these faces is out of the memories of my childhood—the face of an ugly, poor, old woman, a weaver by caste and profession, who lived in our neighbourhood. As a child, it was in her wizened face that, for the first time, I saw the glory of Mother India.

Her name was Hakiman, but she was popularly known as Hakko. When I was attending primary school, she was already grey-haired with deep wrinkles on her dark face. No one—not even the woman herself—knew her exact age, but she had been a widow for more than 20 years. Since her husband's death, she had been working with her own strong hands to bring up her children, carrying on single-handedly the family business of weaving cloth on an ancient handloom, besides doing all the household chores. Old and asthmatic as she was, she would always get up before sunrise. Even in the winter months, while we lay warmly wrapped up in our heavy quilts, we could hear the grinding, monotonous music of the *chakki* from her house. As we passed in front of her door on the way to the school or the bazaar or played in the narrow lane with her grandchildren, we could see Grandmother Hakko (as we were strictly enjoined by our parents to call her) at work—sweeping the floor or plastering it with mud, cooking, washing the clothes of her sons and daughters, grandsons and granddaughters, or seated at her loom, her gout-ridden legs hidden in the pit which all weavers must dig in the ground to keep themselves level with the warp, stretched only a few inches above the ground. As with her dexterous hands, she wove the woof into the warp, the rhythmic beats of the flying shuttle—*khat tana pal nalee*, as we used to mimic the sound—drew all the children of the neighbourhood to Hakko's place. "Grandmother Hakko, Grandmother Hakko," we would tease her, "Where are your legs?" and she would smile indulgently and reply, "My legs are where my wisdom is"—anticipating the popular adage that "a weaver's wisdom lives in a hole". Now that I think of it, I marvel at Grandmother Hakko's remarkable sense of humour. She certainly could laugh at herself.

Grandmother Hakko lived adjunct to our big *haveli* in a kind of shoebox—a tiny mud-walled outhouse with just two small rooms, a narrow verandah and a few square yards of unpaved courtyard plastered with mud. Yet she kept it so clean that in the neighbourhood, there was a saying that in Hakko's house, one could eat parched rice straight off the floor.

Grandmother Hakko would toil from sunrise to sunset, but whenever she came to our place—and it was generally at night—we found her always smiling and in good spirits. What a cheerful old soul she was! Despite her gout and asthma, she had a strong, working woman's constitution. To her dying day, we never saw her back bent. Only some of her *paan*-and-tobacco-stained teeth dropped out, giving her mouth a cavernous look whenever she laughed, giving us children another excuse to tease her. "Grandmother Hakko! Grandmother Hakko! Where have your teeth gone?" To which, of course, she would give the expected reply, "Shall I tell you the truth, children? This is what happened. When I was asleep, some naughty little mice came and ran away with my teeth." In all my life, I have met no one who could laugh at herself so spontaneously.

She was a great favourite with the old as well as the young because she talked so pleasantly and entertainingly, with never a word of malicious gossip or scandal. Whenever we could drag her away from her nightly confabulations with the older women of our household, all the children would gather round Grandmother Hakko and ask her to tell us a story. She was a grand storyteller and, wide-eyed with wonder, we would listen to her tales of three princes, seven princesses, giants that were bigger than mountains and fairies that lived in flowers, horses that had wings and parrots that talked! She could not read or write but she must have had a lively imagination as well as a wonderful memory to have told us all those stories and in such a fine manner.

I am sure she had not heard about the principle of equality between man and woman, and would certainly not have understood if you mentioned Democracy or Socialism. In her naively humorous way, she might have asked, "What kind of bird is that, son?" Yet, she not only did a man's job, observing no *purdah* despite being a Muslim but also dealt with men on terms of absolute equality. Unlike the timid souls brought up in the *zenana*, she was not scared of ghosts or thieves. Poor as she was, she could be polite without the slightest trace of cringing. She could look any policeman straight in the eye, and money-lenders held no terrors for her as she never borrowed money.

Having worked all her life, she had saved a little for her old age. Never having heard of a bank, all her savings (which might have amounted to a ₹100 or ₹200) were in the shape of a few silver ornaments she always wore on her person and even slept wearing them. I still remember her ears bent and the lobes elongated by the weight of the heavy silver earrings which hung in a bunch. She prized these ornaments dearer that life because they represented the toil and scraping and stinting of her whole life-time and the only hope for the future of her children. It had been her ambition that when she had saved enough, she would buy a house and leave it for her sons after she died. It was her supreme purpose of her life, the fixed goal towards which she strove with single-minded devotion.

But one day, to the utter surprise of all of us, she appeared with all her ornaments gone—the bunch of ear-rings, the necklace, the bangles and wrist-bands. But she had the same old smile on her lips and there was not the slightest bend in her back.

This is how she had come to part with her precious ornaments.

Mahatma Gandhi, along with the Ali Brothers, came to our town of Panipat. They addressed a public meeting in my grandfather's house and spoke about the thrillingly new concepts of Swaraj and Non-Co-operation. Grandmother Hakko, too, quietly sat in a corner and listened attentively to the speeches, drinking in every word that fell from the Mahatma's lips. She was particularly fascinated by what he had to say about the significance of the spinning wheel and the handloom and she smiled understandingly when he called them "weapons in our battle for freedom". She knew how to handle these weapons. At the end of the meeting, when collections were made for the Swaraj Fund, Hakko calmly took off all her ornaments and placed them into the Mahatma's "beggar's bowl". Following her example, many other women, too, donated jewellery—a ring here, an earring or nose-ring here, a pair of bangles or a necklace. But there could be no comparison with grandmother Hakko's donation, for she had given away her entire life's savings—and the hopes of her children's future—to the cause of the nation.

Since then, she would come to our house every evening and ask my grandfather for news of Gandhi*ji* and his doings. As the old gentleman read the paper out loud to her, gurgling his hookah all the time, she would interrupt him with some naïve question or other. "When will this rule of the *firangis* end, Khwaja Sahib?" or "How is our Mahatma Sahib's health? He looked very weak and thin when he came here." She would attend all meetings held by the Congress and the Khilafat Committee, not sitting in the curtained-off enclosure reserved for women, trying to understand the political speeches as much as she could. Then she would come to our place and ask grandfather, with a deep sigh, "But will this Swaraj come in my lifetime, Khwaja Sahib?" For the first time, Hakko was concerned with the thought of her death.

Her eyes were beginning to fail and she could work only by touch and by dint of lifelong practice. The gout had practically paralysed her legs and no longer was she able to walk even up to our house. Her sons had told her to give up all work and rest. But she did not give up spinning and, when no one was in the house, she would drag herself to the loom and start weaving. *Khat tana pat nalee*—the shuttle would fly at the command of her practised fingers as we ran up to her. "Grandmother Hakko! What are you weaving?" And her reply mystified us, for she said, "I am weaving a *kafan* for myself." We did not know then what a shroud was but now I know the significance of what she said. In those days, people were buried in shrouds of fine, foreign-made long cloth. But when grandmother Hakko died, her last will was that she should be given the shroud that she had finished weaving only a day before she passed away. She was the first to be buried in a *swadeshi* shroud—a patriot unto death!

Just a few relatives and two or three neighbours accompanied her coffin to the burial ground where she was put to rest in an ordinary grave, without even a tombstone to mark it. I accompanied my grandfather just out of morbid curiosity. There was no funeral oration, no procession, no flowers, no flags, just a nameless old woman buried in a handwoven shroud!

But I wish I knew enough at that age to shout aloud at least one slogan: "*Bharat Mata Ki Jai!* Glory to Mother India!"

2. THE DEFEAT OF MANU

Manu, the ancient lawgiver, classified humanity into four classes—the Brahmins, who were supposed to have been born from the mouth of Brahma, the Lord of Creation, the Kshatriyas from his hands, the Vaishyas from his legs and the Shudras, the lowliest of the lowly, from his feet. Beyond the pale and even more polluted than the untouchables were the *mlechhas*—the foreigners and followers of other religions—who had no place whatsoever in Manu's social scheme.

But does Mother India, who is the Mother Supreme of all the people of this country, also believe in these divisions based on caste and creed? Does she also maintain a distinction between Hindu and Muslim, Brahmin and Shudra? At least, it should not be so because to a mother, all her children equally dear, be they fair or dark, good-looking or ugly, intelligent or dull-witted. But they say that Mother India is illiterate and old-fashioned, steeped in traditions of orthodoxy. Is it possible for her to discard the ancient concept of caste and accept the newer creed of human brotherhood?

Whenever I reflect on this problem, I am reminded of the grandmother of a friend of mine who lives in Poona. The 80-year-old Brahmin lady has witnessed many vicissitudes in her long life. There is a strangely peaceful and serene expression on her wrinkled face as if she has experienced all the pain and pleasure in the world and fathomed the deepest secrets of life, as if there is nothing that is hidden from her and nothing which has any terror for her, not even death! The basic secret of life that she seems to have discovered is that inner peace as well as external harmony spring from the service of others and the abnegation of self.

For as many years as her grandsons can remember, Nani (as they call their maternal grandmother) has been devotedly serving her only daughter's family. At this age, there is not much strength left in her frail body; nevertheless I have seen for myself that she gets up very early, long before anyone else in the house, takes a cold water bath, washes her own clothes, spends half an hour in *puja*, then lights the fire in the kitchen to prepare tea for her grandchildren. On her tottering legs, she climbs the stairs to deliver their cups of tea while they are still in bed.

Nani can speak no other language but Marathi. When she was a child, girls' education was still an unpopular heresy. She has never read the newspapers, nor even listened to the radio, and I don't think she was ever within a mile of a political meeting. She has never raised the slogan, "*Inqilab Zindabad*—Long Live Revolution!" Yet, after a long and weary quest, groping and stumbling through the narrow lanes of Poona, one day, Revolution itself managed to reach the old woman's house. One of her grandsons joined the Socialist underground in the Quit India Movement of 1942. Situated in an obscure by-lane, Nani's house provided an excellent hideout, and so it came to be that the place which once echoed only with devotional *bhajans* now reverberated with conspiratorial whispers of underground revolutionaries. Nani heard strange new words and the serenity of her mind was assailed by disturbing new ideas—Freedom, Revolution, Swaraj, Socialism—but she kept her lips sealed.

After sunset every evening, unknown shadowy figures quietly entered the house, went up the stairs on tiptoe, confabulated in whispers, spent the night there and disappeared the next morning before sunrise. Nani served them as she served her own grandsons—she gave them endless cups of tea, which seemed to be their main diet, cooked for them, washed their cloths and made beds for them. And then, in the silence of the night, as they locked themselves in along with her grandson to plan their dangerous escapades, Nani lit a little lamp before the image of Lord Shiva and prayed for their safety and welfare. She did not know what exactly these young men were up to but she knew they were not ordinary criminals and that whatever mischief they were doing was for unselfish motives. Moreover, her own grandson was involved and her protective maternal instinct blanketed all these nameless friends and comrades of his.

Nani may be illiterate but she is no fool. She speaks little but hears everything and thinks a lot, too. Very soon, she discovered that these nocturnal visitors to her house were not all Brahmins. Many of them belonged to lower castes and some were untouchables and *mlechhas*—Muslims and Christians! But something prevented her from protesting against this flagrant violation of the hallowed rules of caste.

She did not consider it necessary to ask, while offering tea, whether the cup would be touched by the lips of a Brahmin, a Shudra or a Muslim. What had brought about the strange transformation in Nani so that she was not only conniving, but actively abetting, the defiance of the laws of Manu? No one knew. Perhaps even she did not know, for she was acting on a protective impulse which was stronger and more compelling than the social code of a thousand years.

When the boys fell asleep, she would sit near the window all through the night, anxiously, apprehensively wakeful, so that if there was the slightest danger of a police raid, she could warn them in time. One dark night, the police did make a sudden swoop. The boys were fast asleep but Nani was awake, keeping her nightly vigil. When she heard the sound of a jeep stopping on the road beyond the narrow lane, she woke up her grandson and his comrades. By the time the police hammered on the door, the boys had made a clean getaway, jumping from roof to roof. When the policemen searched the house they found no one there except a half-blind, toothless old woman. But the blankets spread out on the floor of the upper room were enough to rouse their suspicions and so they took her to the police station with them. She was subjected to a severe interrogation and cross-examination which lasted for hours. Who were the people staying in her house? Who had slept there that night? Were they not underground revolutionaries? Where was her grandson? Who were his friends and co-workers? Did they hold secret meetings in her house? But Nani had only one innocent answer to all these questions: "I don't know. I am an old, illiterate woman. What do I know of such things?" Not a word that might betray her grandson or his comrades escaped her lips. And, exasperated by her feint of senile innocence, the police officers released her.

Nani's *puja-paath* still continues. She observes all the fasts and misses none of her religious observances. But she no longer practises untouchability. Last year, when her socialist grandson got married and many of his Muslim friends came to stay at her house to take part in the various ceremonies, some of her orthodox relatives were so shocked that they refused to attend the wedding. They tried their best to persuade Nani, in the name of religion and the ancient social code, to exercise her matriarchal authority and order her grandson not to invite his Muslim friends to the more sacred ceremonies of his marriage. But she turned a deaf ear to them, again pleading the helplessness of senility, "I am now too old to interfere or even to care. Let the boy do whatever makes him happy." The next morning when I got up, I saw that Nani was serving tea to my wife and talking to her—with the help of her granddaughter who was acting as interpreter—about much the same kind of things as my grandmother would have done.

Since then, I often wonder if, when the history of India's struggle for freedom comes to be written, the name of the unknown Nani will also be mentioned—the one who renounced her most sacred social principles for the sake of her country's freedom? Then I ask myself: "what gives the strength and courage to this shrivelled-up, old, toothless woman to defy the ancient social code? Is it because she is 'Bharat Mata' and, as such, she is greater and more sacred and more permanent than even the Laws of Manu?"

3. FLOWERS IN HER HAIR, DUST ON HER FEET!

Complacent North Indians—and I used to be one of them—have a set of prejudices and pre-conceived notions about South India which are derived not only from ignorance but also from a superiority complex which must be a racial hangover left behind by our Aryan ancestors. South Indians—be they Tamilians, Andhraites, Malayalees or Kannadigas—are lumped together under the blanket description of "Madrasis" who are all supposed to speak the mythical Madrasi language. Like foreigners, many of us in the North also believe that the caste system in the South is still impregnable and the legend is widely believed that in the South, Harijans dare not walk on public roads, and that if even the shadow of a Shudra falls on a Brahmin, the hapless untouchable is liable to be beaten to death, while the Brahmin, of course, has to immediately cleanse himself with a bath in holy water.

Imagine my surprise, therefore, when my wife and I reached Madras and were received at the station by a friend who promptly invited us to dinner at his place that very night. I know that my friend, though a Brahmin by birth, did not believe in caste taboos. But what about his parents—especially his mother, since women are notoriously more orthodox? Would she tolerate a couple of *mlechhas* polluting her kitchen? Or would they serve us food outside the *chauka*—the sanctified square of ground where they themselves would be sitting for their meals?

Discussing this among ourselves and being prepared for a socially uncomfortable evening, we kept the appointment and arrived at my friend's place just a little after sunset, as he had duly warned me that they dined rather early. His father being out of town, we were received by his mother and two sisters, all of whom greeted us with such cordiality that all our doubts and apprehensions disappeared, and in no time we were feeling quite at home. It was not a Westernised household and we all dined together off banana leaves, sitting on the floor. The old lady along with her children served food to us, and later joined us to take her frugal meal. The laws of caste were broken a hundred times in that single evening as the Brahmins and the *mlechhas* passed the dishes to each other, touched each other while dining and, at the end of the dinner, shared sweets from the same plate and *paan* from the same *thali*!

After that evening, we were in Madras for 10 days, lodged in a hotel. But my friend's mother insisted that we eat every single meal with them. In fact, we spent most of our time in that household and, after a couple of days, we freely moved about the whole place, my wife even invading the sanctity of the kitchen to prepare some North Indian dishes for our hosts as if we were members of the same family.

How did that Brahmin family come to discard its traditional, orthodox ways? That is a significant chapter of our contemporary social history. The father, a theosophical-minded humanist, left a well-paid administrative job (he was then Chief Accountant of one of the largest industrial concerns in the country, drawing more than ₹1,000 per month) to do social service as an inmate of Mahatma Gandhi's ashram.

Since then, the family had been associated with all the movements for social reform and national independence. But their cosmopolitan and unorthodox way of life was not derived merely from their political ideology. As the father moved from place to place on his different missions, the children spent their formative years in many different parts of the country. Madras, Calcutta, Jamshedpur, Allahabad, Wardha, Bombay, Almorah—at one time or other, these places had all been home to them. Inevitably, they became multilingual, too. Tamil, of course, was their mother tongue. But the mother had spent her childhood in Malabar, so she speaks Malayalam quite as fluently as Tamil. For years, they lived in UP, so all of them can speak good Hindi, while Bengali is like a second mother tongue to them. Both the daughter (who studied at Shantiniketan and later attended Uday Shandar's Culture Centre at Almorah) are married to Bengalis—one to a film director, the other to a writer. The grandsons who live in Bombay speak a quaint but charming mixture of Tamil, Bengali, Hindustani, Gujarati, Marathi and English. So this household, having assimilated such a variety of languages and cultures, can really claim to symbolise the unity-in-diversity that is India.

Epitomising this cultural synthesis in her person is the mother, undoubtedly the most interesting and remarkable member of the family. This grey-haired lady, who must have been exceptionally beautiful in her youth, was one of the first women in the South to get a college education, 35 years ago, at a time when it was rare for girls even to attend schools. She not only speaks, but reads and writes Hindustani as well as English. She contributes essays and verses in Tamil to the best literary journals. She is perfectly at home in a gathering of politicians or litterateurs and even though today, she lives in a one-room flat and dresses in coarse *khaddar* saris, she can move without the slightest awkwardness in the highest social circles.

When her husband resigned from his job and joined Mahatma Gandhi's band of *satyagrahis*, she, young and attractive and socially popular as she was, without a moment's hesitation gave up the easy life she had been used to—the huge 12-room bungalow, furniture and servants—and since then has never looked back.

Renunciation such as hers often breeds a martyr complex, not to mention the kill-joy asceticism which so many of our self-sacrificing idealists acquire. But in her case, an innate sense of humour has saved her from any such psychological aberrations. Today, she runs her household without the help of a single servant doing all the domestic chores with her own hands—from sweeping the floors, cleaning the utensils, fetching water, cooking and serving food to her children as well as her children's guests! She is on her feet practically the whole day and far into the night. Yet, there is never a frown on her brow and whatever work she does, there is always a smile on her face. Nor has she lost her former interest in life. Besides the daily newspaper, which she is the first to read every morning (as she is always the first to wake) she regularly reads books and magazines in Tamil, English and Hindi. On most political, social and cultural issues, she has an opinion of her own and can talk intelligently on any current topic. She still attends political meetings, participates in literary discussions and is an active worker of several women's organisations. Her aesthetic tastes are fully developed. A connoisseur of music and classical dancing, she must attend every important recital. She gave her daughters not only college education but also specialised training in music, dance and other arts. She goes to the movies and her criticism of them is trenchant and well-informed.

One of the most remarkable characters I have ever met, she is a rare combination of idealism and practical good sense, of a social conscience and a sense of humour. She and her husband renounced their easy and even luxurious life in the national cause but there is no bitterness or cheerlessness in her character, which is so often the case with our self-consciously conscientious patriots. As *satyagrahis*, her husband, her son and she have all been to jail at one time or another, but she does not parade these sacrifices; she does not even mention them. In sharp contrast with the grim-countenanced "martyrs", a type with which we are all too familiar in this country, she has not lost her natural verve and joy of living. She laughs, and quite often, at herself, plays with children, gets into animated discussions, enjoys good food, likes to listen to good music, and even if she herself wears the coarsest hand-woven saris, she has not lost the usual woman's enthusiastic interest in good clothes. She is nearly 60 years old, yet always active, and though the hair has turned grey and there are wrinkles on the face, her heart is still young and gay. Time, the great destroyer, has not been able to efface from her face the smile which, her contemporaries say, was the most attractive characteristic of her youth and today sums up her entire personality.

I remember one hot afternoon, when all of us were taking an after-lunch nap on cool straw mats spread on the floor, I happened to wake up suddenly and saw that the old lady was wide awake, holding a Tamil book with one hand and, with the other, fanning her grandsons. On her own face, I could see shining beads of sweat. But her mind was occupied with the book, while her heart was in her children. She seemed never to bother about herself. Soon, she would get up, put away the book and make tea for us, then she would fetch water from the pump and bathe the children. I was suddenly struck by the glorious enigma of her personality. How is it that she works so hard and so selflessly and yet never a frown appears on her serene and happy face? How is it that having once tasted affluence and comfort, she is so cheerfully reconciled to a life of voluntary privation? How can she do so many things simultaneously—read a book and fan the children, hum a classical raga while drawing water from the pump, cook *chapatis* and also discuss the pros and cons of Prohibition or the trends in modern Tamil literature?

Then suddenly it dawned on me that she can do all this because she is not an ordinary woman but the Supreme Mother, Mother India, with a book in one hand and a fan in the other, whose hair is adorned with rose-buds and whose feet are covered with the dust of daily toil, whose eyes sparkle with the charm of Bengal and whose lips bear the smile of Malabar, whose body has the grace of Rajasthan and the strength of the Punjab, and who has the serenity of age on her face and the courage and enthusiasm of youth in her heart.

4. THE REFUGEE

The tragic storm of August-September 1947 blew away nearly 10 million people, like autumn leaves, from one end of the country to the other—from Delhi to Karachi, from Karachi to Bombay, from Lahore to Delhi, from Rawalpindi to Agra, from Noakhali to Calcutta, from Calcutta to Dacca, from Lyallpur to Panipat, from Panipat to Montgomery! The thousand-year old joint family system was shattered beyond repair. Age-old friends and neighbours were ruthlessly separated. Brother was torn away from brother. Uprooted from their ancestral homes, millions found themselves transplanted in strange and alien soil.

In October of that year of poignant memories, this very storm blew two frail old women into Bombay, hundreds of miles away from their respective hometowns, One of them was my own mother, the other was the mother of a Sikh friend and neighbour of mine. One had come from the East Punjab and the other from the West Punjab, one from Panipat and the other from Rawalpindi. By a strange coincidence, they reached Bombay on the same day. My mother, along with other women and children of my family, was evacuated from Panipat in a military truck and brought to Delhi. She stayed there for three weeks, huddled in a small room with two other families, and then came to Bombay by plane because it was still unsafe to travel by train. My friend's mother, along with her old husband, came in a refugee caravan from 'Pindi to Amritsar, from there to a refugee camp in Delhi, and finally from there to Bombay.

I called my mother "Ammaan", and my friend calls his mother "Maanji". When both of them arrived here, I discovered that that was about the only difference between these two old women.

Maanji used to live in Rawalpindi in her own house. It was a double-storeyed building, she told me one day. She occupied the upper floor, while down below on the ground floor were shops, mostly tenanted by Muslim shopkeepers or artisans. Many of her neighbours, too, were Muslim. There was a close bond of good neighbourliness between all of them—Muslim or Hindu or Sikh. The Muslim women of the neighbourhood called the old

Sardarni "Behanji", while the younger ones respectfully addressed her as "Maanji" or "Chachi". That was the pattern of living not only in that neighbourhood, not only in Rawalpindi, but all over the Punjab.

The town of Rawalpindi was the whole world for Maanji. She had never been anywhere else. Her son worked first in Lahore, then in Calcutta, and finally in Bombay. But to Maanji, these cities belonged to another, far-off world. If she had her way, she would never have allowed her son to venture far from home. She often argued with him, "What's the use of earning money, my son, when in those cities, you get neither pure milk nor *ghee*, neither apricots nor peaches, neither grapes nor apples. And *baggoogoshas*? Why, in the city they don't even know what that is!" At home they had a buffalo of their own, giving no less than 10 seers of milk every day. After churning the curds to take out butter, she would distribute the buttermilk to the whole neighbourhood. Everyone would thank her and say, "May your son live a thousand years, Maanji"—but that would remind her of her son, eating hotel food in a city, and that would make her sad.

Not far from 'Pindi, they had a bit of their own land leased to some farmers. Twice a year, at harvest time, they would get their share of the produce—wheat or maize or *bajra*. Milk and butter and *ghee* were, of course, available at home. Then there was a small, but steady income from the rest of the shops. And thus they lived—a contented old couple, at peace with themselves, their neighbours—and their God!

When in June 1947, the newspapers published the news of the impending Partition, it did not alarm or even worry

Maanji or the old Sardarji. Politics, they always thought, was no concern of peaceful folk like them. Whether the country was called Hindustan or Pakistan, what did it matter? Their concern was only with their neighbours, and with them, their relations had always been friendly, even cordial. There had been inter-communal riots in the past—"It was a fever of the mind, son, which seized the people now and then"—but never had they been involved is any unpleasant incident. This time, the fire of hate and violence raged more fiercely than ever before, but even then, Maanji was sure that it would soon cool off. Her son wrote from Bombay asking them to come there, but Maanji would not agree to abandon her beloved Rawalpindi. Many of her relations and Sikh and Hindu neighbours migrated to the East Punjab, but she stayed put in her house. Whenever anyone said it was dangerous for Sikhs to live in West Punjab, she would say. "Who will harass us here? After all, the Muslims who live around us are all like my own children—aren't they?"

But then came the influx of Muslim refugees from the East Punjab, embittered and incensed with hate and revenge. The situation in 'Pindi became increasingly dangerous for Hindu and Sikhs and some of Maanji's own Muslim neighbours came to her and pleaded with her to go away to a safe place of safety at least for some time, as they were worried about her safety. And yet, there were some who reassured her and pledged that they would protect her life, honour and property with their own lives. In particular, the old lady remembers the loyal devotion of a Muslim tailor, a tenant of theirs, who kept watch night and day on their home. "May he live long," she always blesses him whenever mentioning him, "he truly helped us and saved us like a real son."

Some of the refugees from the East Punjab were staying in their neighbourhood. Maanji was so moved by their pitiable condition that she voluntarily sent them donations of foodstuffs, clothes, blankets and beddings—and it never occured to her that they were Muslims, supposed to be the enemies of her people, and so she ought not to help them. Nor did she imagine that soon she, too, would be in a plight very similar to theirs.

Them something happened that snapped the last thread of her faith. On the road, in front of her house, a Hindu *tongawallah* was stabbed to death. This is how Maanji described the gruesome incident and her own reaction to it. "Son, it was bad enough that the *tongawallah* was killed. They killed him because he was a Hindu, but they did not spare even the horse. You know a horse has neither religion nor caste. And yet, they went on stabbing the poor animal with their daggers till the poor, dumb creature bled to death. Then I knew the madness had gone too far, and human beings had become something else, something horrible and evil, that we could no longer feel safe in Rawalpindi."

And so she locked up her house, leaving everything behind just as it was. She still did not imagine that she was abandoning her hearth and home forever. The prevalent madness, she hoped, would blow over one day, and then she would return home. "But by the time we reached Delhi," she said with a sigh, "my old eyes saw things—horrible things—both there and here, that told us that we could never again go to 'Pindi." By the time they reached Bombay, the memory of her home in Rawalpindi was only a pain in her aged heart.

In Rawalpindi, she used to live in a house with six spacious rooms, wide verandahs, and a big courtyard. In Bombay, she and her husband live with his son in a single room tenement—with a *dhobi* occupying the room on one side and a coal-shop on the other. There is a small kitchen which also serves as dining room, bathroom and storeroom. When my friend lived there alone, the room was always in a mess—books, newspapers, dirty linen and unwashed tea-cups lying about everywhere. But anyone who visits the same place now finds it completely transformed. Within its narrow limits, everything is spotlessly clean, well-arranged. There are white sheets on the beds with embroidered pillow-cases, the floor shines with constant scrubbing, and there is not a particle of dust or dirt anywhere. In Rawalpindi, Maanji had two men-servants and a maid-servant. Here she cooks with her own hands, washes the dishes, sweeps the floor. But she has a maternal and pleasant smile for any friend of her son who happens to drop in and, of course, she would never let anyone go away without eating something or at least taking a cup of tea. Maanji has lost her hearth and home, all her life's savings and possessions From a prosperous landlady in Rawalpindi she has become a refugee in Bombay, but her hospitality has not lost its North Indian flavour and fervour!

Maanji has a fair complexion, a rather short stature and frail body, her hair which was already grey has turned almost completely white since after the Partition, and her health is not so good. She gets attacks of asthma and neuralgia. But she never sits idle for a moment, never relaxes or sleeps except for about six hours at night. First to get up in the morning, last to go to sleep, throughout the day she is constantly working. Whether it is cooking for her son, or darning and mending her husband's old clothes or making tea or *lassi* for a guest, she insists on doing everything with her own hands. Seeing her, you would never imagine that she is a refugee who has lost and suffered so much. She never proclaims her tragedy. She never curses or abuses those who made her leave her home. She still remembers her Muslim neighbours with affection, and brightens up whenever her husband reads out a letter received from Rawalpindi. Only very occasionally, a soft, cold sigh escapes her lips, as she says, "Your Bombay may be a great and grand city, son. But we can never forget our Rawalpindi—those pears and apricots and apples, those grapes and melons and *baggoogoshas* that you never get in Bombay..."

And suddenly she is silent, tears bubbling up in her tired, old eyes. And it seems that in the intensely human heart of this refugee "Mother India" there is neither anger nor hatred, neither rancour nor self-pity, but only memories— memories that are soft like ripe apricots and fragrant like *baggoogoshas*...

5. A BIT OF INDIA IN PAKISTAN!

In everyone's experience and imagination, the first incarnation of Mother India is one's own mother. Of all Her many faces and forms, this is the dearest and the most familiar.

It was only in the last years of her life that I fully realised the deep humanity, the tolerance, the strength of will and the love of her country that were all along latent in the character of my mother. Till 1947, she was just my mother. Against the flaming background of the 1947 riots, for the first time I saw in her the glory of Mother India.

When the influx of the hundreds of thousands Hindus and Sikh refugees, cruelly uprooted from the West Punjab, reached Panipat, most of the Muslims in our town decided to migrate to Pakistan—all 40,000 of them—all except my mother. When her relations and neighbours pressed upon her to join them in their *"hijrat,"* she stoutly refused. "We shall not leave our country", she said. "My son has decided to remain in India and in this decision I am one with him. I know that it was not easy for her—or for anyone else in her position—to make that decision but out of her inner strength, she made it and stuck to it through a period when many sane minds were losing their balance and many stout hearts were losing their courage.

For 22 days, as the riots raged round Panipat, she remained there alone with her daughters, without any male member of the family. There were periods of curfew when, for a whole week, no one was allowed to move out in the streets. The family servants were gone. There was a stock of wheat in the house—it had to be ground in a *chakki* and chilly-and-onion chutney was all that could be had to eat with *chapatis*. For days, she saw her grandchildren go without milk. Mother was a *paan* addict, but during the curfew, there were days when a single *paan* leaf could be had only for a rupee—so she would buy one and cut it up into a dozen little pieces, and thus pass the day.

I was a thousand miles away in Bombay, and of my two cousins, one was in Poona and the other in Delhi—only 50 miles from Delhi—but even that short journey was not safe in those dangerous days. Letters and telegrams were not being delivered, and all communications between us were cut off. The entire responsibility of the whole family rested on my mother—a chronic invalid, having lived a veiled existence all her 60 years, generally prone to fits of hysterical depression, drugging her asthmatic attacks with doses of Ephederine. Yet, her mind was clear on one supreme issue—she would not migrate to Pakistan. And from some mysterious source within her, she drew the strength of will to stick to that decision. Then, thanks to the kind and timely intervention of Prime Minister Jawaharlal Nehru, a military truck was sent to Panipat to bring our family to Delhi and to send them from there to the comparative safety of Bombay. They had to leave at an hour's notice and could take with them only what the three veiled women could carry in their hands. Like Maanji, when she left Rawalpindi, my mother, too, never imagined she was leaving her home forever. She was sure that, once the storm subsided, she would return to her ancestral homestead. So, locking the main door of our old and straggling house, she had a cardboard fixed to it with the notice that the occupants of that building were not migrating to Pakistan but were temporarily going to their relations in Bombay.

Twenty days they had to live in Delhi before they could secure air passage to Bombay. Meanwhile, news arrived that our house in Panipat had been broken open and looted. Delhi, too, was in the grip of violence—and of fear and hate. Living huddled up in a crowded room, eating when they could, the children often going without milk, with all sorts of panicky rumours current in the city, it must have been quite a harrowing experience. At last, the air passage was secured, and for the first time my mother travelled without her *burqa*—a centuries-old convention blown off by the cruel wind of destiny!

Waiting for the plane at the Santa Cruz airport, I was assailed by a host of doubts and misgivings, wondering how my old and infirm mother had been affected by those grim and gruesome happenings. Would I find her, my mother, too, swept off by the tide of hate and anger and bitterness that seemed to engulf both India and Pakistan? Would I find her mind unbalanced by the vicious atmosphere rampant in the subcontinent? Had she, too, lost her innate humanity, her kind and genial nature, her tolerance and goodwill? Was her interest in life, her wonderful sense of humour, lost forever? She was already infirm and an invalid, she could walk with difficulty. Would she survive the experiences she had gone through? Would she, a nervous case who was scared even by a thunderstorm, survive her first journey by aeroplane?

And then the plane taxi-ed to a stop, and I saw her coming down, her face only partly covered by a shawl, walking slowly, supported by my sister. This was the first time she had ever ventured out of the four walls of the zenana without the voluminous *burqa* with which she elaborately veiled herself whenever she travelled. How many times I had argued with her on this issue, but she had always remained a firm, even fanatical, upholder of the *purdah* system. I had always hoped that one day she would give it up. But I was unhappy on that October morning to see that she had had to discard it at the peril of her life. I feared that this 'forcible reformation' might have further embittered her...

Thinking these thoughts, I escorted her to the car. For a few minutes, she lay back, trying to recover her breath. Then she said something which came as a pleasant shock to me. She said: "After this journey, I have decided to travel only by air. It is much more comfortable than a train." And I felt like giving a whoop of joy for it seemed to me in that moment that life had won a resounding victory over the forces of darkness and despair and death!

And that night, she put all my other doubts and misgivings to rest when she told us of all that had happened in Panipat and Delhi. *"Na ye achchay na woh achchay,"* she summed up the situation with remarkable clarity. "Neither this one is good nor that one. The Muslims are just as bad as the Hindus and Sikhs. There is blood on everyone's hands. But as a Muslim, I blame Muslims—for they brought disgrace to our religion by all that they did."

Riots were raging in Bombay, too. In those days, Mother knew that Shivaji Park where we were living was a predominantly Hindu area. Ours was the only Muslim family in the neighbourhood which had refused to evacuate to a "safe" Muslim quarter. Yet, the very next day after her arrival, Mother put on her *burqa*, took two of her grandchildren with her and went for a stroll along the beach, collecting seashells for the children. Even when I suggested that her going about like that, with her tell-tale *burqa*, might not be safe, she dismissed my fears with a laugh. "*Arrey*, ja!" she exclaimed, "Who will harm an old woman like me?" With complete nonchalance she went on her walk, while I sat on the boundary wall of our house, keeping a nervous vigil. I proved a coward while she betrayed not the slightest sign of fear. Then I knew that her faith in humanity was stronger than mine.

A Hindu refugee friend of mine from the West Punjab was then staying with us. When Mother heard how his parents and sisters had escaped from the horrible riots in Sheikhpura, having had to walk all night up to the border, how they had passed several weeks shivering with cold in an improvised refugee camp, with not even a blanket for everyone, she could not restrain her tears. Then she called me and said, "Look, from today, this boy is your brother. Look after him. Maybe thus we may be able to atone for the sins of our co-religionists." After that, five times every day after namaz, she would pray. "Ya Allah, may all the homeless—be they Hindus or Muslims or Sikhs—return to their homes and may we, too, one day see our Panipat again!"

When the news came of Mahatma Gandhi's assassination, it was as if a death had occurred in our own family. Mother did not touch food that night nor the next day, sitting by the side of the radio, listening to the running commentary on the funeral procession, weeping quietly. As the commentator announced the completion of the last rites, she heaved a deep sigh and echoed the feelings of a whole nation: *"Hai, ab Hindustan ka kya hoga?"*

But the irony of fate did not allow her to be buried in her own country. She went to Karachi to see her younger daughter and there became bedridden with her old and chronic ailments. Yet, to her last breath, she remained loyal to the land of her birth. She knew she might not recover from her illness, but she wanted to die in India. From her deathbed, she had an application sent to the Indian High Commissioner for a permit to return to India. She waited for it every day, as life slowly ebbed out from her body. At last the permit arrived—with endorsement of her Indian citizenship. For a few moments hope revived in her. Like the last flicker of a lamp. She asked for arrangements to be made for an air passage to Bombay. And the next morning she died, still dreaming of returning to her country and her people.

She is buried in a Karachi graveyard. But her soul, her memory, the ideal of her life, are with us in India.

And six feet of earth in Pakistan will forever be Indian soil—for buried in it is my mother, who also was Mother India!

RICE

Twisting like a serpent, creeping at a snail's pace, buzzing like a swarm of bees, two long queues—one of men, the other of women—were advancing towards the government grain shop. The women's queue was even longer than the men's—quite a furlong in length, with its tail-end in a narrow alley round the street corner. Late-comers were taking their places behind each other. They did not get even a glimpse of the grain shop. All that could be seen was the head of the woman in front.

Several hundreds of women—Hindus, Muslims, Parsis, Christians, Jews, Muslim women, veiled and unveiled, fisher-women with black, shiny, healthy bodies, the fragrance of the flowers in their hair mingled with the unmistakable small of fish, bare-legged Goanese women in frocks, Anglo-Indian girls in artificial silk stockings and high-heeled shoes, reeking of cheap scent and powder. Plump, dark-eyed Jewesses with flowered shawls around their shoulders. Slim and lissome Marathi women, the tight grip of their saris revealing the contours of their bodies, and pale-faced Gujarati women who were either too thin or too fat. Wives of clerks, wives of mill-workers, wives of taxi-drivers, wives of petty shopkeepers, married wives and unmarried wives. Faded jasmine and fish; coconut oil; scent and perspiration. And in the heat of the noon-day sun, the vapours of these varied smalls rose and dissolved into an unseen cloud of summer languor. Marathi and Gujarati, Hindustani and English—a babble of tongues, the buzzing of a million bees. The slow tortuous eternity of time. Sixty seconds make one minute. Sixty minutes make one hour. One hour, two hours, three hours. And, twisting like a serpent, creeping at a snail's pace, buzzing like a swarm of bees, this long queue of waiting women became longer every minute. By the time one woman at the head of the line left with her portion of the grain, two or three more joined in at the rear. Two hundred women, two hundred and fifty women. How patiently they had been waiting since the early hours of the morning. When one leg was tired, they just shifted their weight to the other. A strange demonstration of patience, devotion and faith, like worshippers waiting for the gates of the temple to open. The new temple! A temple to which Hindu and Muslim and Christian had come, devotees all, each with a bag in her hand and but one thought in her head. One thought, one desire, one passion—one paylee of rice.

Durga came and joined the queue at the far end. Today, she was later than usual. She had got up in the morning with a severe pain all over her body. She did not feel strong enough to go to the grain shop and wait for hours in the queue, but there was no alternative. There was not a handful of rice in the house. For the past two days, they had been getting their meals from the bazaar. Today the grain shop was opened after several days. If she did not get her ration today, then God alone knew how many days they would have to wait. And, meanwhile, if it should happen...if her baby should arrive....

Durga's husband worked in a mill. He left home early in the morning and returned home at nightfall, limp and exhausted after slaving at the machine all day. Durga did the household shopping. She did not mind it in the least. For a working-class woman it was neither a disgrace nor an ordeal. As long as she lived with her parents in the village, she had always helped her father in the fields, sat at the spinning wheel, ground corn on the hand-mill, chopped fodder for the cattle, milked cows, washed them and collected their dung for fuel. After she came to the city with her husband, she also went to work in the mill like her Nandoo. In the evenings, she cooked their meals because her husband did not like bazaar food. But she never imagined for a moment that she was over-worked. For her Nandoo, she would do anything. How good he was! How many wonderful places and things he had shown her—Zoo, Chowpatty, Apollo Bunder with real big ships going out to strange and distant lands across the black waters. He had often taken her to the cinema where so many wonderful things happened—where the gods and goddesses and saints she had heard of came magically to life, all on a simple white screen. In the village, Durga could never have dreamed of such things.

Nandoo was always considerate to her and very kind. He never came home drunk on paydays like other mill-workers, nor did he ever beat his wife. Before the sixth month was over, he stopped Durga from going to the mill. "You should not work now. You should stay at home and rest. After all, you are going to be the mother of my son!" That is what he had said, his eyes twinkling with joy. "Look here, Durga. You must give me a son. I don't want a howling female infant."

Twisting like a serpent, creeping at a snail's pace, buzzing like a swarm of bees, the queue of women was slowly advancing towards the grain shop. Now, about a dozen women had fallen in behind Durga. Discussions were raging along the line. A Parsi woman was exhaustively commenting on the rising prices. A Khoja woman was blaming the Congress for the scarcity of grains. A Christian woman thought it was all Mahatama Gandhi's fault: if he had not provoked the government, the government in its turn would not have felt it necessary to punish the people by putting all these restrictions on food-stuffs.

"Why do you blame the Congress and Mahatmaji?" a plump, grey-haired Gujarati matron intervened, "Don't you know the government has sent out millions of tons of wheat to Iran, Iraq and Egypt?"

"Yes, we know the government has sent much grain out of the country," countered a Maratha woman, "but we Indians are not blameless either. Look at these baniyas! They have hoarded up enormous stocks which they will sell later in the black market at fancy prices."

"Exactly, exactly. We have to stand in queues for five and six hours for one miserable paylee of rice while these baniyas have got thousands of mounds hidden in their underground cellars waiting to be sold at three times the old price."

"Such ill-begotten scoundrels should be hanged."

"That is done in other countries. Here, the government fives them titles of Rai Bahadur and Khan Bahadur. They get fatter and fatter on war contracts." Another group was discussing the latest war news.

"Oh, my sister, you don't know. This 'German' and 'Jaapaan', they are the same. If 'Jaapaan' gets a chance he will certainly attack Russia."

"A jackal runs to the city when his death is near! Take it from me, if 'Jaapaan' attacks Russia, his days are numbered. This is not Burma or the Philippines that he swallowed and did not even belch afterwards. This Russia is Russia."

"Russia." Standing in the sun, Durga's head started to swim but she thought to herself, "I have heard this word 'Russia' somewhere." She did not know why, but there was some close relationship between her and this Russia. Then she remembered. Nandoo had once taken her to a workers' open-air meeting. About 30,000 workers, men and women, sat on the ground in the big maidan. Durga had never in all her life seen so many people together in one place. She felt lost, as if she were a drop in the ocean. On every side, there were red flags and on the flags was a white sickle like the one which her father used during the harvest and a white hammer like the one she had seen the blacksmith wield to beat the red-hot iron. In the centre of the crowd was a raised platform from which people were addressing the meeting. And Durga was astonished to find that though the man was speaking on the platform, his voice came from a big, black, trumpet-like thing fixed to a wooden post just near her. Even the voice was like no ordinary human voice. It was as if someone were speaking down into a well. And this voice was saying, "Brothers and sister, the bloodthirsty wolves of Hitler have attacked Russia—Russia, the homeland of the workers of the entire world; Russia, the only country where the peasants and workers rule... The workers of the world should stand up to defend Russia.' And then, shouts of "Soviet Roos zindabad" burst from 30,000 throats and Durga feared the heavens would fall.

How long had she been standing in the queue? She turned around and saw about 20 women in the line behind her. Now she had come to the street corner and by craning her neck a little she could even see the red signboard of the grain shop. But nearly a hundred women still stood between her and her paylee of rice. "Why does this shopkeeper take so long to measure out the rice?" she wondered as she shifted from one tired leg to the other. Overwhelmed by the heat, the other women, too, had grown weary of talking. A policeman in his funny blue uniform rested against the tree on the opposite pavement, his eyes closed. Perhaps he was asleep. Looking at him, Durga felt all her tiredness, all the ache in her legs, all the gnawing pain in her abdomen concentrate into her eyes. She felt like lying down on the cool-looking pavement and going to sleep. In a dizzy moment, she reeled but saved herself from falling by clutching the shoulder of the woman in front of her.

"Oh my sister, why can't you stand on your legs?" It was a gentle old woman and there was no anger or malice in her reproach. But Durga felt so ashamed that she became nervous. Stepping back, she was stung by a sharp tongue. "Are you blind? You have crushed my foot!"

and as this woman pressed backwards to release her foot from the weight of Durga's body, there was a series of curses and exclamations in several different languages right down to the end of the line.

Durga felt terribly humiliated. She clenched her teeth, trying to steady herself, and fixed her eyes on the ground. At one moment, she almost decided to leave her place in the queue and go back home without the paylee of rice. But then she thought of Nandoo and what he would eat in the evening; her dear Nandoo who was doing several hours "overtime" these days for her sake. Besides, by now she had moved quite near the shop. It only she could get through another half-hour, she could go back with the rice in her bag.

But why this terrible pain—as if someone were sawing her in half? She was perspiring so much that it seemed as though she had taken a bath with her clothes on. Her head swam and she felt giddy. And inside her, waves of excruciating pain ebbed and flowed. She felt as though she were being stabbed again and again with a sharp dagger. Had the much-awaited moment, arrived for which she had been so ardently hoping? But it couldn't be. Only three days ago, the midwife had assured her that it would take another two weeks before she would deliver. This must be some other kind of pain.

Thinking, hoping, despairing, resisting the storm of agony that threatened to engulf her every moment, she somehow managed to keep on moving with the queue. At last, she was in front of the grain shop, only one woman ahead of her. But when this woman went in to receive her portion, Durga saw that she would have to climb up two wooden steps that led to the shop. And these steps, each of which was a foot high, appeared to her like the 120 steps one had to climb to reach the temple on the hill near her village. Would she ever be able to climb those rickety steps?

The woman came down from the shop, smiling triumphantly, wiping the perspiration from her face with the end of her saree. The woman behind Durga gave her a not-very-gentle push. "Come on, you there. Get going. Are you sleeping?" The baniya looked at Durga and said, "Come, Bai, hurry up. There are so many others waiting." But he did not see that her face was growing pale and her legs were trembling at the very thought of having to climb those steps.

"I...I...I won't be able... Brother, please give me my rice here." Her lips were dry and her voice almost choked.

"Why? Do the feathers of the surkhab adorn you that I should treat you differently? Come up and take your rice like all the rest."

"Come on, get going."

"If you don't want it let the next one be served."

At every step, she expected to stumble and fall. But, somehow, she managed to drag her body into the shop. Trembling, she held out the bag to the baniya and gave him the coins she had clutched in her hand for the last four hours and which were wet with perspiration. The baniya picked up his measure and, filling it with rice, emptied it into Durga's bag. Then Durga saw that the fat baniya was revolving in a very strange manner. The measure, the bag of rice...the whole shop was revolving. Going round and round and round—the whole shop, the sacks full of grain, the tins of ghee, the oleograph picture of the monkey god Hanuman on the wall hit Durga in the face and she screamed.

She found herself buried under a huge pile of rice. She was being suffocated. But then, the rice on top of her was removed by unseen hands and she breathed again. She saw the god Hanuman filling the measure and emptying it into the bags of the waiting women. He was saying, "Here is a paylee of rice for you. Here is a paylee of rice for you," and his famous long tail was dancing with joy. But no, it was not Hanuman's tail. It was a serpent with the face of the woman who had abused Durga. All at once, the serpent began to bloat and become longer, reaching all the way from the shop to the street corner. And now it was crawling and wriggling towards Durga. The serpent took a deep breath and Durga felt herself irresistibly drawn into the monster's belly.

But actually it was not the serpent's belly. It was a dark room. Dark and stifling. Not a breath of fresh air. She again felt suffocated. From its unfathomable darkness, someone cried, "This is India! This is India." And the two red lights were burning brightly in the distance. Durga thought they must be the eyes of the serpent, but when they came nearer, they were two red flags with the sign of the hammer and sickle. Now there was light everywhere. Thousands of workers were marching, singing a song in some strange language. From inside the well came a booming voice, "This Russia is Russia." Suddenly, dark clouds hid the sun. There were flashes of lightning and the roar of thunder, but it turned out to be the booming of guns. Bombs and shells were falling everywhere as she had once seen in the cinema. A bomb fell just near her and she was blown to pieces...

Durga felt she was lying stark naked and was ashamed. But before she could get up, a frightful giant came and started cutting her body in two with a huge saw. When she looked again, it was Nandoo himself. Merrily he was sawing her and saying, "Look here, Durga, you must give me a son!" And thousands of people gathered around and, seeing her in this plight, started laughing. One of them said, "This is India." But the fat Gujarati woman said, "Why do you blame Gandhiji? He himself is being starved by the English."

Everyone disappeared and Durga saw that she had become fat, fatter even than the baniya, and she had a bulging stomach. Then someone thrust a big, sharp needle into her stomach and she started bleeding so profusely that all her clothes were dripping blood. Far away, someone was knocking on the door of her mind. Some people were talking. Still revolving, the shop was emerging out of the clouds of unconsciousness. Slowly, it came to rest. The picture of the god Hanuman still hung on the wall. Feeling weak and exhausted, Durga could not turn her head to see the people who, she felt, stood around her in the shop. They were talking but she could understand only a few words.

"...poor woman...perhaps it is her first..."

"...strange are the ways of God..."

"...fancy, in such a place..."

"...some labourer..."

"...get out, all of you. This is not a tamasha."

Durga felt a strange emptiness within her. She moved her hand and found that all her clothes were wet. Water? Perspiration? No, blood! And a horrible thought flashed through her mind.

"Here...in front of the whole world...I have delivered a child. Could anything be more shameful?" She would have liked the earth to open there and then and swallow her up with her infamy! Death was better than such disgrace. A wave of weakness swept over her and, closing her eyes, she thought, "How shall I go from here! How shall I ever be able to face people again? Everyone will point at me in the streets!"

For several minutes, she floundered in this consciousness of shame. Once again, she was about to succumb to a state of coma when...

A baby cried.

A baby? Whose baby? Her baby! Durga's child! Nandoo's child!

And this tiny little voice in a moment swept away all embarrassment, all shame. The clouds of weakness and unconsciousness cleared from Durga's mind. Disregarding her pain, she turned her head and saw the tiny bit of pink flesh that lay bundled up in some rags. From its little mouth emerged the cries that only a mother understands. "It must be hungry," she thought and started to loosen her blouse.

The dignity of motherhood shamed petty curiosity and everyone walked out of the shop, smiling.

After some time, Durga got up, supporting herself against the wall and, with trembling but triumphant steps, she walked out. With one hand, she supported her son. In the other was her bag. And in the bag was one paylee of rice.

AJANTA

"Ajanta is the eternal source of inspiration for India's art… There is nothing like it in this world… Even Englishmen and Americans are rendered speechless here… These caves are 15 centuries old. It took 800 years to dig and carve them out of this hillside, to paint these gigantic frescoes and to make these thousands of statues… Look at this image of the Buddha…"

The well-worn voice of the official guide rose sharp and clear in the vast hushed cave and echoed back from the lofty ceiling. In return for a monthly salary of ₹28 and some ₹2 tips, he repeated this commentary several times over, every day of the year. Repeated it mechanically, unvaryingly. The same thing over and over and over and over again. Like a trained parrot, or a gramophone! To Nirmal, the guide's voice seemed like the steady hum of a spinning wheel or the buzzing of a bee.

Never-ending, meaningless, soulless!

But Bharati, who was an art-lover as well as a specimen of art herself, was listening to the guide with rapt attention. She wanted to merge with this hallowed shrine of ancient art. Every painting, every sculpture, every pillar and cornice inspired her, provoked her to burst out into loud exclamations of joy and wonder. "Nirmal, look at this... Nirmal, look at that... Look, what a divinely peaceful expression on the face of the Buddha! Look, what a strange coiffure this *apsara* has! How sweet! How wonderful! How utterly beautiful!"

Nirmal was silent. He was not listening. Neither the mechanical hum of the guide, nor Bharati's exclamations of joy made any sense to him. His eyes were on the frescoes, no doubt, but he saw nothing apart from dim, futile patches of colour. He didn't even know which cave he was in or which painting he was supposed to be admiring.

The interminable, meaningless commentary of the guide continued. "Look at this painting. Here is Mahatma Buddha in one of his earlier incarnations, delivering a discourse to his disciples. And this is a court dancer who is listening to the Exalted One. She is late for her dance at the palace and when, from her, the Raja learns of this strange mendicant and his strange preachings, he goes to test the Blessed One, 'Who are you?' the Raja demands to know, 'And what do you preach?' The Buddha replies that he is Nobody and is giving a discourse on Truth and Peace. Hearing this, the Raja orders his executioner to cut off the hands, feet, nose and ears of the *sanyasi*. But every time the executioner's sword came down, the Buddha said, 'But Truth and Peace are in my heart, not in my hands or feet or in my ears or nose.' Look at his wounds, how the blood..."

Blood!

Out of the interminable, meaningless harangue of the guide, only this word made sense to Nirmal.

Blood!

Like a hammer-blow, this word struck at Nirmal's subconscious mind.

Blood!

The stone walls of the Ajanta caves suddenly melted into nothingness. Now, there was nothing—neither frescoes nor sculptures, neither Bharati nor the guide, neither green hills nor the picturesque little stream. Art and History, Religion and Ethics, the Buddha and the cruel Raja of Benares—in an instant, everything and everybody had melted into nothingness.

Blood!

Streams of blood! Rivers of blood! An ocean of blood! And, carried on the crest of these bloody waves, Nirmal was flung back on the shore of Bombay. The same blood-stained Bombay from which he had escaped to these caves, 300 miles and 1,500 years away.

The first of September. As usual, after finishing his day's work, Nirmal had gone to his friend Vasant's office in Girgaum so that they could go home to Dadar together, when someone brought along the news that a communal riot had broken out in the city. Pushing their pens, pencils and typewriters aside, the entire staff started discussing the situation.

"Don't you worry. This riot will be brought under control in no more than a few hours. The Government is fully prepared for all emergencies this time..."

"But how did the trouble start today? The Muslim League black flag demonstration was announced for tomorrow..."

"This is all due to the news of the Calcutta riots..."

"I hear the police has unearthed several thousand knives and daggers..."

"I hear some Muslim Leaguer was trying to place a garland of old shoes around a portrait of Pandit Jawaharlal near Golpitha..."

Just then, the clanging bell of an ambulance was heard from the street below and everyone ran to the windows. Some casualties of the riot were being taken into Harkishen Das Hospital across the road. A shortish, stout man who was wearing a striped shirt, dirty *dhoti* and black Maratha cap went up to the gatekeeper of the hospital and enquired: "Who were they? Hindus or Musalmans?" The gatekeeper, who had already contrived to peep into the ambulance as it went in, replied: "One Musalman, two Hindus." And immediately, agitated, excited voices began to whisper in front of the "Hindu Hotel".

All the shops along Charni Road had been closed by then. Even the "Hindu Hotel" had pulled down its shutters—only the iron grill that protected the main entrance was partly open. The last empty tram had clattered away an hour ago. No cars. No taxis. No buses. The road was deserted. But clusters of people leaned out of upper floor windows—waiting, watching, grimly, silently expectant. There was a peculiar tension in the atmosphere, like a tightly stretched drum waiting to be beaten into a fearful tattoo.

Suddenly, footsteps were heard approaching from the Sandhurst Road side. Silently, automatically, almost simultaneously, all pairs of eyes turned around in that direction. It was a thin young man in *kurta* and pyjama, walking along at a carefree pace, looking quite oblivious of the bloody happenings in the city.

"Look at this bastard—walking along merrily as if it was his Bhendi Bazar!" hoarsely whispered one person from the crowd in front of the "Hindu Hotel". Immediately, the smallish, stout man in the black cap started looking for something under his shirt.

The young man was now passing under the window of Vasant's office. Nirmal could see him from close quarters as he went by. Darkish complexion, sensitive, intelligent face. Thin, very thin. One could almost count his ribs sticking out under his muslin shirt. A student, or maybe a clerk. Nirmal didn't know why, but he felt like shouting aloud a warning: "*Miyan bhai*, look out as you go along. These are very bad times." But no sound came from his lips. And in a flash, he knew it was already too late, as a sharp, long knife rose in the air, catching the rays of the sun on its shining blade.

The next moment, the knife had plunged into the young man's back—right up to the hilt. Automatically, the poor wretch raised his hands—perhaps to protect himself against the cowardly attack—but the next moment he reeled and fell to the ground. And a low moan escaped his lips which was at once a cry of protest and his death-rattle.

"*Haai Bhagwan!*"

And there was consternation among the group in front of the "Hindu Hotel".

"*Arre!* This seems to have been a Hindu!"

"Don't you worry—the bastard must be pretending, hoping to save his life."

"How can a Hindu be wearing a pyjama?"

"Open his trousers and see if he is circumcised."

The knife was still in the young man's back but, not bothering about that, several people went ahead and turned the body over. One of them pulled at his pyjama cord.

Nirmal turned away his face out of shame. He felt polluted, as if someone had rubbed his face into a pile of filth.

When he looked again, the examination was over and the murderer was calmly pulling the knife out of his victim's back after restoring the body to its original position.

"Mishtake ho gaya!" he said and, tearing a strip from his dirty *dhoti*, began wiping off the blood from the knife blade.

As the knife emerged from the wound, Nirmal saw a little stream of red-black blood spurt out of the wound and give a splash of colour to the dead man's white clothes. It then spread over the tarred road.

Blood!

"Blood and hate and strife—how remote they all seem in this quiet, peaceful haven!" Bharati spoke softly, tenderly placing an affectionate hand on Nirmal's back. With a violent jerk, a tidal wave swept him out of the sea of blood.

"What…er…what did you say, Bharati?"

"I was saying that in these caves, we seem to be far, very far, from the bloodshed of Bombay and Calcutta. Thousands of years distant! I am sure here, at last, you will be able to forget all those horrible things you have seen in Bombay…"

Poor, naïve Bharati! Bharati! Who was a lover of beauty and a beauty herself! How much she bored him! How empty was her head!

She dearly loved Nirmal and could not bear to see him unhappy even for a moment. The very day the riots started, she knew that Nirmal's delicate and sensitive mind would not be able to bear the ghastly sights. After the murder on Charni Road, which he had witnessed with his own eyes, for three days he could neither eat nor sleep. It was as if he had been struck dumb. A vast, oppressive silence had descended on his mind and heart. Afraid of being dubbed a sentimentalist, he had not confided the reason for this to anyone. But he always unburdened his soul in Bharati's presence. and related to her the entire sequence of horrors. "I can still see that thin, young man throwing up his hands in his last futile gesture of self-protection. His desperate scream is still ringing in my ears. That agonised look of his haunts me day and night. And even when I sleep, I dream that he is drowning in a sea of blood and I cannot go to his rescue."

And gently, affectionately caressing his mass of wavy hair with her soft, tapering fingers, Bharati said, "My poor Nirmal!"

How assiduously she tried to soothe her tormented friend! But everything—the cinema, the radio, music, even her conversation and her love—failed to distract his mind from the remembrance of the ghastly spectacle he had witnessed. Nirmal had suddenly lost all his former liveliness, his famous sense of humour, his keen and intelligent interest in all the multifarious aspects of life. He came, as usual, to see Bharati every day. But for hours he just sat mute without uttering a single word, his horror-stricken eyes fixed on some invisible spectres.

She would say, "Nirmal, my darling, I know your sensitive soul has been deeply wounded. But, for God's sake, don't let yourself drift into a morbid state. That

Charni Road episode was horrible, no doubt. But you must try to forget it."

And he would say, "Yes, it is better to forget." And to himself he would add, "If only one could forget."

Nirmal Kumar was gifted with a tender and imaginative mind. He was a poet as well as a prose writer of some distinction among the younger men of letters. His verses, lyrics, essays and stories appeared in the leading literary magazines of the country. Bharati, daughter of a millionaire, connoisseur of art and patron of artists, was a great admirer of Nirmal's literary genius. If she could, she would have got a pretty little bungalow made on the top of a pine-covered hill for him—far from the madding crowd, away from the intrusions, disturbances and excitement of life—and in that Olympian retreat enshrined her literary god to communicate with the Muses, undisturbed by anyone. But to Nirmal, this ivory-tower conception held no appeal. He was a reporter in a daily newspaper. Bharati often said that for a promising writer on the upgrade, it was a criminal waste of talent and time to adopt journalism as a career. But Nirmal held that in present-day India, creative literature was a luxury few could afford. Journalism was at least some sort of a profession, even if it was so poorly paid. Moreover, as a reporter, he came face to face with life in all its significant and dramatic aspects. In courts and police stations, in strikes, processions and public meetings, he got an opportunity to observe and study humanity and human character, both in its collective and strictly individual manifestations. And it was these observations which his creative instinct later transformed into essays and verses and stories which were distinguished by their awareness and truthful depiction of the basic realities of life.

As a reporter, Nirmal had to roam through the city even during curfew hours.

Sandhurst Road.

Bhendi Bazar.

Pydhonie.

Byculla.

Parel.

Dadar.

The whole of Bombay was an armed camp seething with hate and violence. Stabbings and murders were being reported from everywhere. Here, a Muslim bakery-man was killed! There, a Hindu milkman was fatally stabbed by a Muslim! Here, a Pathan was pounded to death! There, a Poorbi-*bhaiyya* was murdered! Here, someone had cut the throat of a 10-year-old boy! There, a lad of 11 had knifed a pedestrian!

The whole city was partitioned into "Hindu Bombay" and "Muslim Bombay". No Muslim dared pass through Pydhonie. No Hindu ventured into Bhendi Bazar. Pakistan and Akhand Hindustan! At last they had been achieved!

Along with other reporters, Nirmal often went on rounds of the "affected areas" in police or military lorries. One day, a white sergeant said to him, "So you Congressmen didn't want Pakistan. Well, today, does a Pakistan exist in Bombay or not?" Next day an English Tommy taunted the group of reporters: "You shouted to us: Quit India. Now that we are ready to quit, why do you all run after us, pleading with us to stay? The Hindus want us to save them from the Muslims; the Muslims want us to defend them against the Hindus. But both agree that they depend upon us, our guns and planes for their safety. Today they both shout: DON'T QUIT INDIA!"

And to Nirmal, it seemed as if the magnificent edifice of Indian freedom had suddenly crumbled like a house of cards, as if all the patriotic traditions of a hundred years had been betrayed and defiled.

The first confused, bloody upheaval of 1857.

The agitation against the partition of Bengal.

Non-co-operation and Khilafat. Swadeshi and Boycott. Gandhiji and the Ali Brothers.

The memorable martyrdom of Jallianwala Bagh. The mingling of the blood of the Hindu and the Muslim and the Sikh for the common cause of Freedom.

Bhagat Singh and his brave comrades. Satyagraha and Civil Disobedience. A flag going up on the banks of the Ravi.

All national songs and all patriotic slogans.

India's Unity. India's honour and self-respect.

Indian art, Indian literature, Indian music and poetry and painting and sculpture.

Everything great, everything noble and inspiring, had been trampled to dust.

"Trampled to dust through the centuries—and yet Ajanta shines like eternal gold." The guide was still rambling on.

"Ajanta is the imperishable masterpiece of Indian art and literature, poetry and painting," Bharati was gushingly enthusiastic.

But in that dark cave, even in the circle of light thrown on the wall by the guide's torch, Nirmal saw nothing but a few pointless blotches of colour. Neither beauty nor art. Neither meaning nor message! Nirmal's heart was heavy with unfathomable anger, a terrible frustration. If he could, he would have liked to shout aloud: "Why all this...these caves, these sculptures, these frescoes, this art, this endeavour? Why? What for? It was all a colossal waste of human effort! A stupid and pointless episode in the long story of man's evolution! It would have been better, far better if, instead of wasting so much effort on carving images out of stones, it had been used towards humanising human beings so that they would not be killing each other today like bloodthirsty beasts of the jungle! India has never learnt anything from Ajanta except the lesson of escape. Escape from the world, from reality, from truth, from life! Ajanta is not only a monument of futility but a Great Lie, a forgery and a fraud..."

Meanwhile, oblivious to the dangerous trend of Nirmal's thoughts, the guide went on with his commentary. "Look at this fresco. The Buddha, mounted on a white horse, is passing through the street. How serene he looks! And look at these women. How devotedly they watch the Blessed One. "

And Bharati was saying, "Nirmal, look at these women. Their faces simply aglow with faith. Truly, none but the artists of Ajanta have fully understood and revealed the true spirit of Indian women, their peace-loving souls, their delicacy, their instinct of motherhood."

The true spirit of Indian women!

Their peace-loving soul!!

Their delicacy!!!

Their instinct of motherhood!!!!

Nirmal felt like bursting into a peal of laughter that would echo through the caves and make the very rocks tremble with the impact of his derision.

The true spirit of Indian women? Their peace-loving souls? Their delicacy? Their instinct of motherhood?

Lie! Fraud!! Deception!!! Dangerous self-delusion!!!!

One day, there was a commotion by the roadside and everyone ran to the windows. Looking out they saw an old, white-bearded Bori Muslim lying sprawled across the tram track in a pool of blood. He had been stabbed in the back. And on the balcony of the building opposite, a group of Hindu women stood, watching gleefully and giggling uproariously, as if they had just witnessed a highly amusing episode in a rib-tickling comedy.

"Look, Kamla," one of them was chuckling, "look at the old *Mussalla*'s beard. From white, it has become red," and all of them joined in the laughter.

The real spirit of Indian women! Their peace-loving souls!! Their delicacy!!! Their instinct of motherhood!!!!

A Red Cross ambulance came hurtling through the street, screeched to a stop and carried away the old Bori who had probably passed away by now. Then a woman came out carrying a bucket of water, which she poured on the road to wash away the big patch of clotted blood.

For several days, Nirmal's ears rang with the raucous laughter of those women and his dreams were haunted by the blood-dyed white beard of the Bori which fluttered eerily like a phantom bird. And it seemed to him that all the women of India were laughing aloud at some grim and obscure joke which was beyond his understanding and sense of humour!

The true spirit of Indian women!

Their peace-loving souls!

Their delicacy!

Their instinct of motherhood!

Several of Nirmal's friends were Muslims. But he could not visit them in their homes during the days of the riots. Then one day, he learnt that his colleague and fellow reporter, Hanif, was a lonely bachelor with no one to look after him and so he decided to go to Bhendi Bazar where his friend lived in a chawl.

When the bus reached Crawford Market, all the Hindu passengers got off. Nirmal was dressed in an English-style suit and at a glance no one could say whether he was Hindu, Muslim or Christian. Indeed, because he was so fair, many thought him to be a Parsi. And yet, as the bus entered deeper into "Pakistani" territory, he had a sinking feeling and his heart began to beat faster with fear. Once, he was almost sure that the hefty "*goonda*-looking" Muslim sitting next to him would hear his tell tale heartbeat and recognise him to be a *kafir* daring to encroach on the territory of the Pure and Faithful. Any moment, he might whip out a shining blade from his jacket and plunge it into the back of the *kafir*—just as the *goonda* on Charni Road had killed a Hindu youth by "*mishtake*"! And for no reason at all, Nirmal felt an itching sensation in his back, near the spinal cord, and an imaginary knife slowly sinking into his ribs.

When he got down from the bus near JJ Hospital, he saw his would-be stabbers on every side. Who knew that the hawker at the vegetable stall might decide to peel off a Hindu pedestrian's skin with the same knife he was using to cut and chop cauliflowers! That bearded Pathan must, of course, be in search of a *"kafir baachcha"* to earn his free entry into paradise with its hordes of *houris*! Behind him, Nirmal heard footsteps and turned round to see that it was a woman in a *burqa*. For a moment, he heaved a sigh of relief but then a cold sweat broke all over his body as the idea struck him that the *burqa* could well be a convenient camouflage for an armed *"goonda"*. And, suddenly breaking into a run, he clambered up the steps of the chawl where his friend lived.

Hanif lay unconscious in a delirium and Nirmal had to stay with him the whole day. When the fever subsided slightly and the patient was able to drink a little milk, Nirmal decided to go back to his lodgings. But just then, they heard a policeman on a bicycle shouting through a megaphone that a 24-hour curfew had been imposed from 5 p.m. and warning everyone not to stir out because military patrols had orders to shoot at sight. There were only 10 minutes for the curfew to begin, so it was out of the question for Nirmal to return to Shivaji Park. He decided to spend the night with Hanif.

Hanif's room was on one side of the building. The little balcony overlooked the main road while the windows opened out on to a side street. There was a rush-hour stampede and everyone was going home in a hurry, fearful of the curfew and the "shoot at sight" order. Nirmal saw a Poorbi milkman whose top knot proclaimed that he was a Hindu, with his brass milk pots dangling from a bamboo pole, rushing along but discreetly keeping to one side of the road. There was fear in the furtive looks he cast to the right and the left as he dragged the heavy load on his shoulders. Again, as when he had seen that young man walk to his doom on Charni Road, Nirmal had an acute premonition of evil. He wanted to shout and warn the milkman. But once again, the words froze on his lips and, in the twinkling of an eye, three toughis waylaid the poor, dark, thin Poorbi.

"Eh, you, son of a *kafir*! Where do you think you are going?"

The poor wretch gave no reply. Perhaps he knew that they were not going to spare him, whatever he might say. Perhaps he saw his death beckoning him from the three pairs of eyes glaring at him. He turned around—only to find another group barring his retreat.

Nirmal's sensitive nature had never been able to bear the idea of *shikaar*. But now he knew what a hunted deer must look like. He saw that look of terror, born of the certainty of immediate death, on the face of the little milkman. He cast one last, hopeless, helpless look in the direction of his pursuers and then made a pathetically futile bid for safety by running into the side street. And in hot pursuit after him went the three human bloodhounds!

Nirmal ran to the other side of the room. But before he reached the window, he heard the milkman stumble and fall. The metal pots crashed on the ground with a brassy crash and the milk flowed across the road in a white stream. By the time Nirmal could look out of the window, the milk had been stained red with the milkman's blood.

"The bastard wanted to run away!"

Nirmal heard a woman laughing in the adjacent room. "*Aree* O, Gulbano, come here, come quickly, a *kafir* has been killed in our lane." And then a chorus of excited feminine voices—young, old, middle-aged and childish!

"*Arrey*, look at the *chuiya* on his head!"

"Serve him right! The Poorbi *bhaiyyas* always add water to their milk. Now he has been properly punished."

"At last our people are beginning to take revenge for the Muslims killed in Girgaum. They won't let a single *kafir* pass through Bhendi Bazar alive!"

One of the women went in and brought out the refuse-bin, which she emptied on the road. A shower of egg shells, potato peelings, banana skins, stale meat and bones, fell on the very spot where flies had already begun to swarm over the little pool of blood and milk.

The real spirit of Indian women! Their peace-loving souls!! Their delicacy!!! Their instinct of motherhood!!!! The echo of the inhuman laughter of the woman on Sandhurst Road merged into the bloodthirsty chuckles of the women of Bhendi Bazar, and this symphony of horror rang in Nirmal's ears wherever he went, whatever he did, even when he slept.

He heard the same grim echo even in the caves of Ajanta. Among these dim, faded and yet vivid paintings he saw a demoniac and murderous expression on the face of every *apsara*, every court-dancer, every woman. And Nirmal's heart filled with a vast, fathomless hatred. "I hate every woman," he was thinking, "every woman—even Bharati." Bharati! Bharati, who loved him and whom he loved! Bharati, who, out of her father's wealth, wanted to build a wall of gold and silver to keep the sensitive Nirmal safe from the ugly and cruel realities of life! Bharati, who had practically "kidnapped" Nirmal to take him away from the atmosphere of hate and violence and bloodshed! Bharati, who would do anything for the man she loved! Love! Love? Nirmal could have laughed.

Love. Hate. Love and Hate! Hate and Love!!

We are brothers. We are lovers. We are friends and comrades!

We are bound by relations of love. Yet we hate each other. We stab each other. We throw stones and bombs on each other. We set fire to each other's homes. We kill each other's children. We cut each other's throats. We love each other!

"Look, look at these dead bodies—the heads have been cut off!" The guide's interminable commentary went on.

He was now perspiring with exertion but his voice showed no signs of strain. And Bharati—the delicate, sensitive, soft-hearted Bharati had turned pale at the sight of death, even in pictures! "This is the cruel Raja," the guide continued, "who has got all these God-fearing folk beheaded and their bodies thrown to be eaten by vultures."

And a quite horribly irrelevant idea crawled into Nirmal's mind: "Perhaps the Rajah was really not cruel at all. Perhaps he liked vultures so much that, to feed them, he got all these people killed. The slaughter he ordered was at least a boon to those evil birds..."

Dead bodies!

Twenty-seven cold, convulsed, decomposed. Dead!

Nirmal had gone to the hospital in the course of his daily rounds when he learnt that the latest batch of fatal casualties had just been brought to the morgue. For them, even death was not final. And now, lying on the cold stone floor, they awaited the last indignity of a post-mortem examination and the Coroner's verdict. And yet there was only one verdict that anyone could pronounce on them: DEAD!

Only once before had Nirmal ever seen dead bodies like these—in the surgical ward of the Medical College where one of his medico friends had taken him.

Here, there were no less than 27 dead bodies. Old men. Young men. Women. Children. Thin, rickety, dried-up bodies. Stab wounds in the back. Intestines oozing out of slashed abdomens. A head severed from the neck, lying near the body—an irrelevant appendage.

Who was Hindu? Who was Muslim? In the fraternity of death, they were one. Who was young? Who was old? Who was rich? Who was poor? The assassin's knife had equalised them all, laid them together on this cold stone floor.

This cold stone floor!

So this was their Pakistan and this was their Hindustan!

This futile death! These vacant, sightless, lifeless eyes! This grim solitude!

So this was their freedom, this was their Islam, this was their Vedic dharma!

Har Har Mahadev! Allah O Akbar!

Nirmal always tried to avoid contact with practical politics. He worked as a reporter for a living but essentially he was not a man of action. His world was the world of thought and feeling. Yet, on the very third day of the riots, he had joined the Peace Brigade of his locality. And perhaps because every public organisation—be it a Peace Brigade, a Seva Dal or an Anjuman Khuddam-e-Watan—needs publicity, and he was connected with an important daily newspaper, he had promptly been elected a member of the Executive Committee. Nirmal's friend and neighbour, Ahmad, was also taken on the Committee, being the only Muslim in the Shivaji Park area, who had joined the Peace Brigade, and such organisations could not obtain official recognition unless they had representatives of both communities on them.

For some days, Nirmal was kept busy and engrossed in the administrative work of the Peace Brigade and he felt that at last he would be able to overcome that oppressive feeling of inertia and utter helplessness that had been produced by the riots. By joining and working for the Peace Brigade, he felt the same exhilaration that soldiers on the battlefield get when they fight—a battle between the forces of light and darkness, of peace and destruction. He was an enlisted soldier in the Army of Peace, participating in a crusade against devilish fanaticism and bestial violence. He might not come out a valorous hero but at least he had the satisfaction that he was doing his duty, that his life had not become entirely futile and barren.

Several times, Bharati coaxed Nirmal: "Come, let's go away somewhere—far, far from here. We'll come back when the riots are over." Agra! Delhi! Kashmir! Ajanta! Ellora! Mysore! Ceylon! She tempted him with every place he had ever wanted to visit. But Nirmal felt it would be extreme cowardice and dereliction of duty to leave Bombay at such a time. In vain did Bharati argue with him that for a sensitive, creative artist like him, it was a criminal waste of his God-given gifts to risk his life in such dangerous days. But he would not listen. And, except office hours, he devoted all his time to the work of the Peace Brigade.

The work of the Peace Brigade? Nirmal had imagined it would be to propagate peace, that the members of the Committee would go from house to house and persuade people of both communities to live in peace with each other, to counteract the propaganda of hate that had already been started on both sides and to create an atmosphere of goodwill and unity. The city, even their own area of Shivaji Park, was being flooded with poisonous rumours:

The Muslims of Mahim are going to attack the Hindus of Shivaji Park!

The Hindus of Shivaji Park are going to attack the Muslims of Mahim!

Hindu milkmen are poisoning the milk they sell to Muslims!

Muslim greengrocers are injecting poison in the tomatoes and cabbages they sell to Hindus!

Don't buy sweets from Hindu confectioners. There is poison in them!

Rumours. Lies! Lies!! Lies!!!

A tidal wave of lies and bitterness and hate which threatened to drown the whole city! Nirmal and Ahmad had hoped that the first business of the Peace Brigade would be to check this avalanche of dangerous lies but soon they learnt how wrong they were.

The work of the Peace Brigade? First—to collect funds! With Ahmad, Nirmal went around to all the flats in the section that had been allotted to them. The few

Muslim residents flatly refused to give any donations or even pay the nominal monthly subscription of one rupee per flat.

"We know what the Hindus are planning behind the camouflage of this Peace Brigade. We have kept Pathan watchmen for our protection."

Some of the Hindus said, "What can your unarmed volunteers do in a real case of emergency? We are keeping Sikh watchmen," adding in a whispered aside, "The Sikhs are allowed by law to keep *kirpans*, you see."

Anyway, the money was collected and 20 watchmen were employed on ₹50 per month to guard the locality during non-curfew hours. The question of fixing their places of duty came up before the Executive Committee.

"Put a guard at each road-crossing."

"Place a cordon all round the locality."

"No, no, that would be silly. After all, the attack can come only from three sides—Mahim, Worli or the sea-side. So we should concentrate the guards only on these sides. In case of attack...?"

"Attack? Attack by whom?"

"The Muslims, of course. These are the only three routes by which they can attack."

"And what are these guards to do?"

"They must be told to keep a sharp lookout for any of them. As soon as they see one, they must blow a whistle so that people can rush to the spot..."

"Only Muslim *goondas*? Aren't Hindu *goondas* also to be apprehended?" Nirmal put out this question but couldn't look into the eyes of his friend Ahmad as he heard the reply from one of the senior members of the Committee. "Let's face realities, Mr. Nirmal Kumar. A *goonda* means a Muslim *goonda*."

After the meeting, he said to Ahmad, "I don't know how you can bring yourself to work with such people. To me, they all seem to be fanatical Hindu Mahasabhaites."

And Ahmad said, "There are any numbers of such blind fanatics on both sides. You don't know the rumours that are being spread among the Muslims of Mahim. They are all convinced that our Peace Brigade is an armed force that the Shivaji Park Hindus are organising to lead a surprise night attack on the Muslims of Mahim."

And so the work of the Peace Brigade went on.

Donations!

Volunteers!

Guards!

Uniforms!

Whistles!

Meetings!

Resolutions!

Applications to the Police Commissioner!

But what about the propaganda for peace and unity? No effort for it, no sign of it! Then what was the purpose of the Peace Brigade, of all this fuss and running, about?

"Muslim *goondas*!"

"Hindu *goondas*!"

"Keep stones and brickbats stored in your home!"

"I have ten *lathis* in my flat!"

"My neighbour has a pistol!"

"We will kill the Muslim bastards, let them come!"

"We will make mince-meat of the Hindu *kafirs*. Let them come!"

Peace! Peace!! Peace!!!

"There is peace and serenity in every stone of these caves," Bharati was saying. "If we come here every day, I am sure you will be able to forget the horrors we have left behind in Bombay."

And the guide was saying, leading them to yet another cave, "You have seen all the caves. Only one remains. But in this you will not find any masterpieces of sculpture or painting. Here, the ceiling, floor, columns and pillars, everything is incomplete. For some reason, the work on this cave remained half-finished..."

Half-finished work? Hadn't he, Nirmal, too, left his work in Bombay half-finished? In fact, less than half-finished! The battle had hardly begun when he had acknowledged defeat.

That last meeting of the Peace Brigade Executive Committee!

Nirmal, from the beginning, had proposed that instead of engaging illiterate and mercenary watchmen and guards, they should maintain a small contingent of the former members of the Indian National Army. They were men of sterling character and patriots proved in battle and could be depended upon to be above communal prejudices. Moreover, they greatly needed and eminently deserved help. So Nirmal was very happy when, at this meeting, the Secretary reported that the old batch of watchmen had been dismissed and in their place 14 INA men had been employed. Now, he felt sure, the Peace Brigade was beginning to work on the right lines. But the very next moment, his optimism was rudely shattered.

An old Maharashtrian lawyer asked, "Is it true that among these INA men, there is one Muslim, too?"

The Secretary replied, almost apologetically, "Yes, but only one..."

A fat Gujarati *seth* cleared his throat and declared, "This has caused considerable misgivings in my section."

A thin, rickety Marwari exclaimed, "This is horrible, absolutely horrible!"

The old lawyer raised his voice, "I want an explanation from the Secretary. Why was a Musalman engaged as one of the watchmen?"

The Gujarati *seth* gave his verdict: "If this sort of thing goes on we will not donate a single pie."

A short, stocky doctor testified, "This is also what people in my section are saying."

The dried-up Marwari shouted, "This is a matter involving our women's honour."

And the old lawyer burst out, "I demand an explanation..."

The President sharply rapped the table, "Quiet, quiet!"

The Secretary tried to stem the tide. "Personally, I don't think there is any harm in our employing this Muslim. There are no communal distinctions among the men of the Indian National Army. But if the Committee so desires, we can get rid of him on some plausible pretext."

"Exactly!"

"At once!"

"Why was he engaged in the first place?"

"There should be no delay!"

Only Ahmad was silent and kept on smiling.

And, seeing him smile, Nirmal could contain himself no longer. Suddenly, something snapped within him.

"No! No!! No!!!"

He shouted with such vehemence that the Secretary, who was writing in the Minutes Book, "Resolved unanimously that no Muslim be employed among the INA personnel..." jumped in his chair and dropped his pen. A big blot of ink appeared where the text of the resolution was being written.

"No! No!! No!!!" As if simply by reiterating his opposition 10 times, he would be able to cancel the other nine votes. "I can never support this resolution. Never! Never!! Never!!!"

For a few moments, the very suddenness and force of Nirmal's outburst silenced the other members. But in that silence, his own voice sounded hollow and meaningless. "Such a resolution would be a disgrace to us, a betrayal of the ideals of unity and peace that we have been professing. Are we to fight communalism by turning communalists ourselves? If this resolution is passed, it shall be my duty to place the whole matter before the press and the public."

And Ahmad continued to smile, as if he was saying "Bravo, my boy! But your gallant words are useless."

The spindly-legged Marwari began, "Mister Nirmal doesn't know that we Hindus are in great danger..."

The fat Gujarati *seth* exploded, "It is no use mincing matters. If this Muslim is kept as one of the guards, we won't give any more donations."

The short, stocky doctor threatened, "We will all resign and join the Sarvrakshan Dal of the Hindu Mahasabha."

But the old, wily lawyer, cool as ever, silenced the rest with a wave of his hand. Then he directly addressed Nirmal. "Tell me one thing, Mister Nirmal. This is predominantly a Hindu locality. Suppose something happened to this poor Muslim while patrolling, who would be responsible for his safety?" Then he triumphantly winked at the Gujarati *seth* and the doctor as if to say, "Do you see how a little legal trick of mine has floored this chip of a boy?"

Ahmad looked at Nirmal. "Didn't I tell you there was no use?" he seemed to say.

The resolution was passed while Nirmal sat, still fuming in his heart. He could have said much, even made an impassioned speech. He could have argued, summoned reason and logic, patriotism and consideration of humanity to his aid, but now he knew that it was futile to smash one's head on this impregnable, solid wall of ignorance and hate and fanaticism. All round him, a sea of voices kept on surging, resolutions were discussed and passed, the members and office-bearers exchanged the usual hot words.

Nirmal said nothing!

Nirmal heard nothing!

His mind became peopled with horrors.

Calcutta!

Bombay!

Ahmedabad!

Noakhali!

Bihar!

The Punjab!

Rawalpindi!

Lahore!

Murders of Muslims!

Murders of Hindus!

Streams of blood, rivers of blood, an ocean of blood!

Hate and violence, violence and hate!

Dishonoured women!

Orphaned children!

Piles of corpses rotting on the streets, stuffed into sewers, and vultures fattening on human flesh!

Leaping flames of a thousand fires rising up to the sky and turning it red. Blood-red!

The whole country, steeped in blood and scorched by fires, splitting into two amidst the triumphant, sarcastic laughter of the foreigners.

And like a mechanical hammer, the thought kept striking his consciousness: "All this is happening because the members of the Shivaji Park Peace Brigade are not prepared to tolerate a solitary Muslim member of the INA."

Suddenly, it occurred to him that all the heroism and glorious achievements of Netaji Subhas Chandra Bose and his Indian National Army had been in vain. The whole struggle for freedom had come to nought. The efforts of all the patriots and the sacrifices of all the martyrs had been futile. All patriotic slogans, all national movements, all national leaders—everything and everyone—were useless! The Shivaji Park Peace Brigade was useless. Nirmal's work for it was futile. There was no point in him remaining in Bombay. There was no point even in him staying alive. And all because communal labels—this one is a Hindu, that one a Muslim!—had proved to be more important than ideals of freedom and unity.

At that moment, the members of the Peace Brigade Executive Committee appeared to him to be demons of ignorance and prejudice and hate, who were staring at him with flaming eyes, who were advancing menacingly to kill him and everything he had ever believed in. Not these 10 alone, millions of such demons were closing in on him from all sides. Among them there were demons with beards and demons with sacred tufts, Muslims as well as Hindus, Bengalis and Biharis, Punjabis and Maharashtrians, Pathans and Poorbis, Gujaratis and Sindhis. All of them thirsting for his blood!

"Run for your life!"

Nirmal's palpitating heart sounded an alarm.

"Run! Run! Run for your life!"

Nirmal not only ran away from the meeting even before it was finished, but the next day, with Bharati, ran away from Bombay.

"Where shall we go?" Bharati asked him.

"Anywhere," he replied, "where there are no riots and no bloodshed, no newspapers and no radio, no Hindus and no Muslims, where there are no knives, daggers, bottle bombs, no burning houses, and no fanatical mobs, no *goonda*s and no *mawali*s. Far, very far! Far from the world, far from life!"

After pondering for a moment, Bharati announced their destination.

"Ajanta!"

Ahmad came to see them off at the station. As the guard blew the whistle, he said to Nirmal, "It's good you are going out for a change. Relax for a few days. But remember, next Sunday we are having a general meeting of the Peace Brigade and I propose to place certain important suggestions before the members. I am sure we will get a better response from the public than we get from the old fogies of the Committee."

The train had begun to move when Nirmal said, "I am never again going to have anything to do with the Peace Brigade." But Ahmad reminded him, running along with the train, "No, Nirmal, no, we cannot leave this work unfinished."

Unfinished work!

What did he care? One did as much as one could and no more. Hadn't these indefatigable sculptors and painters of Ajanta, too, left their work unfinished? After 800 years of interminable labour, what had happened that they were forced to leave this last cave incomplete? A question that challenged one's imagination!

"What do you think, Bharati…?

But Bharati was not there. Nor was the guide! Nirmal's voice bounced back from the ceiling and, echoing through the gallery that ran round the cave, returned to him.

Perhaps, engrossed in his thoughts, he had got lost in some dark corner of this vast, shadowy, incomplete cave and Bharati and the guide, imagining him to have left, had gone out to look for him on the terraced path that ran in front of the caves. Not finding him there, they might even have concluded that he had walked back to the *dak* bungalow.

Nirmal must have lingered among the shadows of the cave for quite a few hours because, looking out through the entrance, he saw the hill across the valley, completely silhouetted by the setting sun. Like a mounting, suffocating depression, the gloom in the cave was deepening very fast.

With a last look around the cave, Nirmal was about to step out when he saw a lighted torch coming towards him.

But the next moment, his amazement was complete when he saw that the man with the torch was a monk clad in a yellow flowing robe. And he did not seem to be in search of anyone. Whatever he might have sought he had certainly found long ago. There was complete serenity about his bearing as he walked with unhurried steps to one of the incomplete pillars and, placing the torch in a hole drilled into the stone, produced a chisel and hammer from the folds of his robe. Then, completely oblivious of a stranger's presence, he started chiselling away.

Nirmal was about to take a step in the direction of the monk when he was held back by the sight of a group of other monks with shaved heads and yellow robes emerging from the shadowy nowhere at the back of the cave, stepping out of solid rock!

Not one of them so much as glanced at Nirmal. All of them took out their implements and started work on the walls, pillars or ceiling—hammering, chiselling, carving! Some began to plaster the walls with layers of fine mud, preparing the smooth surface on which later artists would paint their frescoes. The vast, vaulted cave rang with the sound of metal striking against stone.

For some minutes, Nirmal watched this amazing spectacle. Then he could contain himself no longer and walked up to the monk who had arrived first.

"Excuse me for interrupting your work, but I must say I am amazed to see you all at work."

"Why?"

"Because I thought this cave would remain incomplete forever."

"The world, too, is still incomplete. Man himself, having yet to evolve to the stage of perfection, is incomplete. But they must be completed."

Nirmal did not fully comprehend this mystifying reply. So he asked, "For how long have you been at this work?"

The monk answered.

"Nineteen hundred years? You mean you are as old as..."

"Before me, it was my father and before him, it was his father...one generation after another. Like the wheel of karma, the cycle of work must go on revolving."

"Your name?" Nirmal tried to give a personal turn to the conversation.

"My name? Nothing. We are all nameless."

It occurred to Nirmal that nowhere in these caves had he found an artist's name painted or engraved. Could artists be so impervious to immortality?

"Then why do you all work so hard?"

"One does not work for anything. Man must work to fulfill his destiny."

"Then how long will it take to complete this work?"

"Who knows!"

"This cave ...."

"...will take 200 years more to complete. Then another cave must be started. And after that still another ...."

"Will Ajanta never reach completion then?"

"Yes—when Man will achieve perfection!"

Nirmal's cynicism at last overcame his sense of wonder and he asked with unconcealed sarcasm, "Please explain to me why thousands like you, for thousands of years, have been wasting your time and talent on this work?

Why? All these caves, dug into the bowels of this hill, all these paintings, these sculptures and carvings—why? And what for?" In his voice, sarcasm gave way to bitterness and anger as he burst out, "It would have been better, much better, if this colossal effort had been spent not on carving stones but on creating human beings so that today millions of us are not engaged in killing each other. You have fashioned these enchanted caves to cheat us and mislead us and to weave a spell of beauty to keep our minds in chains. These caves are the escapists' paradise, tempting us, encouraging us to run away from reality, from truth, from life!"

On the monk's face was an unruffled calm and the merest touch of a smile in which there was no trace of malice or bitterness. Only love and pity—and a deep understanding. Without taking off his eyes from his work, he replied, gently, softly: "No, my friend."

Nirmal was infuriated by the serenity and the ever-smiling countenance of this man. He shouted, "What then is the purpose of Ajanta? What is the message of Ajanta?"

"Listen."

And, saying this, the monk resumed his work. In the hall, there was perfect silence, but for the rhythmic sound of metal striking stone!

Nirmal waited for the yellow-robed craftsman to deliver a sermon on the philosophy of Ajanta, the meaning of Ajanta, the message of Ajanta. But not one word more escaped his lips. Only the sharp metallic click-click-click of his chisel. And thin wafers of stone kept softly falling on the ground like leaves in the autumn wind.

"Then the message of Ajanta..."

Suddenly, a gleam of understanding flashed in the darkest recess of his mind and the sentence remained half-formed on his tongue.

There was complete silence in the vast, vaulted cave. Only the rhythmic sound of metal striking stone. This, then, was the message of Ajanta which the monk had asked him to heed.

Seeing the dawn of understanding on Nirmal's face, the monk serenely smiled and resumed his work. But Nirmal felt that he had stumbled on the greatest treasure of the earth. The Philosopher's Stone or even the Elixir of Life was nothing compared to his precious secret. He had got the Message of Ajanta.

He did not know for how long he sat in a corner, listening to the sound of metal striking stone.

Click-click-click!

And every time the chisel struck the stone wall, to Nirmal it said: "Work! Work!! Work!!! Effort! Effort!!Effort!!! Endeavour! Endeavour!! Endeavour!!!"

It is human effort that chisels stone, that cuts slices out of solid hills, that creates beauty out of the bowels of the earth. It is human endeavour that puts the colour of life into paintings and moulds images of life out of rocks. It is human endeavour that raises Man above beasts. Work is worship. Work is its own justification, its own reward… Click! Click!! Click!!!

The rhythmic sound of metal striking stone. Tomorrow, if not today, in 200 if not a 100 years, some day, these stones shall be chiselled into shapes of beauty and art. Not a few, but thousands, shall carry on this work—generation after generation! This work will never be completed. For its aim is the perfection of art.

Click! Click!! Click!!!

The rhythmic sound of metal striking stone. Tomorrow, if not today, in 2000 if not a 1000 years, some day, human nature shall be chiselled, carved and embellished with beauty and grace and art and knowledge; not a few, but millions, will participate in this process—generation after generation! This work will never be completed—for its aim is perfection of humanity.

Click! Click!! Click!!!

The rhythmic sound of the chisel falling on stone. The monk was so engrossed in his work that he did not even know that he had hit his thumb with the hammer. As he saw drops of fresh, red blood falling on the stone floor, Nirmal remembered all the paintings and frescoes he had seen in the caves. Even after thousands of years, how fresh and brilliant were the colours! And the quaint idea struck him that instead of paint, the artists must have used their own blood. Perhaps that was why they were so alive with feeling.

Perhaps he drifted into sleep. Perhaps he was lost in thought.

When he awoke, he found the cave lit up by the slanting rays of the morning sun. But it was quiet like a graveyard. There was not a soul in sight—neither those sculptors, nor the painters. Even the torches had disappeared.

Then, had he dreamt it all? Perhaps…what a strange dream!

"Must have been a dream," he decided, "in this pervading atmosphere. No wonder my imagination conjured up such a fantasy."

But on his way out, as he passed the pillar which that dream monk had been working on, he saw a newly carved lotus flower that was not there the previous evening. Or was that too a trick of his imagination?

Then he remembered something and looked down on the floor. There they were, glistening like rubies—several drops of fresh, red blood!

Without meeting Bharati at the *dak* bungalow, Nirmal walked straight to the railway station. The next day was Sunday and, riots or no riots, he had to be in Bombay to support Ahmad's proposals in the meeting of the Peace Brigade. There was no escape from the riots, from Bombay, from life!

In the train, a fellow passenger asked, "Have you been to Ajanta?"

And Nirmal replied, "No, but I am going towards Ajanta."

COLD WAVE

In the dense fog, thought Baldeo, the lights of Connaught Place are like yellow leprous sores on the dark face of the night. Then he became aware of a tremulous litany that was barely audible above the silky swish of the cold night breeze.

The old beggar, huddled in a corner with his bundle of rags, was whining in the mendicant's familiar monotone. "This accursed cold is killing me, *Baba*. Give a blanket to a helpless old man, *Baba*. May Bhagwan bless you and your children, *Baba*." And because he was blind, he did not know that Connaught Place lay deserted in the cold and foggy night like a doomed and dead city. There was not a soul to be seen moving around anywhere. The sightless old wretch had heard a rustling around and hopefully concluded that it was a charitable pedestrian but it was only an old newspaper crumpled into a ball and blown by the wind through the stone-flagged arcade.

Baldeo caught hold of it with a desperate fling of his arm, hoping that the sheet of paper might serve as a shield against the inexorable chill. He had heard somewhere that in cold northern countries, the poor folk used old newspapers to wrap around their bodies under their flimsy shirts. Maybe that night he would do the same. But when he unrolled the ball of paper he found, it was riddled with windows gaping through every column where someone had neatly cut out bits of news for advertisements. A sieve, he bitterly reflected, cannot serve as a shield! Then, idly, he turned over the paper in the pale glimmer of the fog-bound street lamp. It was only two days old, and one of the surviving headlines declared: "COLD WAVE HEAVY TOLL, WILL HIT DELHI TOMORROW."

"NEW DELHI, Friday. North India continues to be swept by a cold wave and reports of more deaths are pouring in from all over the region. Within the next 24 hours, Delhi will also be in the grip of a severe cold wave, which is travelling down from the snowbound heights of Simla. Apart from the hundreds who have been frozen to death, many cases of pneumonia due to exposure have been reported..."

Baldeo did not need read any further. He could write an even more exhaustive and poetic report on the current cold wave. The fog was like an icy shroud thrown over the capital. Every morning, one could see the thin layers of frost over the ponds and the tanks. With the minimum temperature touching freezing point, people were sleeping under as many as three blankets and a heavy cotton-padded quilt. But the deadliest of all, mused Baldeo, is the breeze blowing down from Simla. He never knew that it could be cold like ice, sharp like a razor blade, and viciously, devilishly, omniscient and omnipresent. For the homeless, there was no escape from it. Wherever you tried to hide, it searched you out in every corner, behind every wall, across every threshold. It found you and then, like a probing icy lancet, it went through your shirt, through your very skin and slashed at your very bones.

I should write some verses about the cold wave," thought Baldeo. Maybe a *ghazal* in one of the shorter metres of Ghalib. If he died of exposure—and there was now every chance that he would—at least his poetry would live after him. It seemed that in such a cold wave, not only the blood in one's veins got congealed, but the very source of inspiration—the grey matter in the brain—is frozen into a block of unfeeling ice. "If the temperature keeps falling during the night," he thought, "and this breeze straight from an icy hell does not slacken, then soon all my senses, my memory and my mind would be stricken by a cold paralysis. I must do something. I must speak something. At least keep on muttering like the poor old man huddled in the corner.

"But, no, I am a poet; an educated, cultured, sensitive young man, not a blind old beggar that I should be whining in a voice like the moaning of a street cur stricken with asthma. But, maybe, my voice too is like the moaning of an asthmatic cur. Maybe, if I speak, my words too would come out whining and trembling with cold. I must say something, just to make sure the cold has not atrophied my vocal chords."

So he said, "Old father, whom are you asking for alms? There is not a soul here for miles except me." Now he felt that his teeth were chattering and his voice, too, was like a moan. And he who was blind did not see—he could not see—that the one who spoke to him out of the eternal dark night was an obviously well-to-do young man in a silk shirt and woollen trousers. The beggar sensed the proximity of a rival claimant for whatever alms might be had that night. What chance had he, with his sightless eyes, against this one who obviously could see and, therefore, more successfully pursue the would-be alms-giver? So he picked up his bamboo staff and his bundle of rags and, groping his way with the end of his stick, went down the crescent-shaped arcade till the night swallowed him up.

Suddenly, Baldeo was struck by the sense of loneliness which was no less vicious than the bite of the freezing wind. Loneliness, too, he thought, is like a kind of chill. Or maybe the cold is itself a kind of loneliness. Where you are alone, without a friend or beloved, no one to talk to, to share your thoughts and feelings, when there is no rush and bustle of the crowded marketplace, then that solitude, too, has in it the freezing touch of doom. Some people believed in that rather than the flaming hell, where sinners would be laid naked on blocks of ice. And even worse was the third kind of hell where every sinner would have to live in solitary confinement. And to Baldeo, at that moment, it appeared that his own private hell combined both the tortures of cold and loneliness. His body, already shivering with cold, was shot through with the sudden realisation that he was alone in a cold, unfriendly, unfeeling world.

"I must do something," he thought, "or this cold—and this solitude—will drive me crazy. I must speak something, but there is no one to speak to. I must at least *think* something, otherwise my idle brain will freeze and then crack, just as the thin layer of frost frozen on the surface of a pond breaks at the slightest touch of the morning breeze. In a little while, I may lose my senses and even forget who I am, where I am, why I am, what I am.

"Who am I? What am I? I am Baldeo Raj Sharma. I don't believe in castes and creeds but since birth, I am stamped a Brahmin. I am a graduate (Literature and Political Science) from Meerut College. My father earns four or five thousand rupees a month from legal practice. Before Independence, he was known as Rai Bahadur Ranbir Raj Sharma, BA, LLB, Advocate High Court. Now he is only called *Pandit* Ranbir Raj Sharma. But I am not just the son of my father. I am also something and someone in my own rights. I am 5 ft 10 in tall and I have an athletic figure. People say I am quite handsome. My friends even believe that I have a better personality than some of the Bombay film stars. My professors have more than once testified to my intelligence and my literary flair. True that I got only a second class in BA but that was because I spent so much time on extracurricular activities, debates, tennis tournaments, amateur dramatics and *mushairas*. I am regarded as a promising young poet with the pseudonym "Nirmal". In the *mushairas*, they call me Janaab Nirmal Meeruti; in Kavi *Sammelans*, I am known as Pandit Nirmal*ji*. They say that my Urdu *ghazal*s and Hindi *geet* are marked by an intimate and urgent sense of passion which is not to be found in any other young poet.

"Where am I? And why am I where I am? Why am I not in my father's bungalow where, even at this moment, the fireplace in my bedroom must be lit, waiting for me. On the double spring bed there must be a pile of soft blankets and a silken *lihaaf* padded with three seers of the finest cotton wool. Under the pillow must be lying my silken sleeping suit and my embroidered *pashmina* dressing gown which I bought in Srinagar last year. In the bookshelves, also waiting for me, must be all the fine editions of the world's great poets—Milton and Byron, Kalidasa and Ghalib. And hidden behind these books, that half-empty bottle of brandy.

"I am not in my cosy bedroom. I am not even in the draughty *boudoir* of Radha, where at this very moment, there must be singing and dancing—and drinking! All the gay young gallants of Meerut must be there—all except me! And Radha, perhaps, must be singing one of my *ghazals* or *thumrees*.

Radha! Radha, whom I loved with such devastating intensity that I left my house for her sake. My father threatened to disown me but I did not care. I left the house just as I was sitting there in a garden chair on the lawn; I did not stop even to put on a sweater or jacket. My mother cried aloud to stop me, but I did not pay any attention to her. I hardly heard her pleading and her wailing—in my ears resounded only the magical jingle of Radha's anklet-bells. I had decided to prove that a poet not only talks about love, he also experiences it and can sacrifice anything in the world for it. Romeo and Juliet, Laila and Majnu, Charudutta and Vasantsena—these are only legendary lovers, figments of forgotten fables. But Nirmal and Radha, Radha and Nirmal—we would become a living legend of love in our own times!

"And so I walked out of my father's house and, just as I was, only in my shirt and trousers, walked through the bazaar to Radha's first-floor flat with its professional balcony overlooking the street. At that moment I was not at all conscious of the cold weather. The afternoon sun was pleasant and warm, in my veins was the hot blood of youth and my heart was aflame with the fever of love. I was sure (because she had often assured me) that Radha too was consumed by the same fire of love and that she would do anything for me.

"Seated in front of her dressing table with a glowing brazier by her side, she was drying her long silken hair after a bath. The fire in the brazier had cast a warm, pink glow on her wheat-brown face and to me it looked like a face illuminated by the inner fire of love. I thought that anyone who was lucky to have her love could never complain of cold weather or of the chills of a hostile world.

"Come, come, Nirmal*ji*," she greeted me with a professional smile, but as she looked up at me, I saw the unmistakable glow of love in those big, black eyes of hers.

"Radha," I blurted out without any introduction, "I have left my house forever."

"Left your house?" she asked incredulously. "But why?"

"Because of you. Father had threatened to disown me because I said I would marry no one but you. Come, we will go to Delhi this very minute and get married there..."

"And if you are disowned by your father, how shall we manage to live?"

"I will get some job. If you like, you can sing for the radio."

"Oh, what a simpleton you are, Nirmal*ji*. Don't you know no professional singing girl is allowed to sing for the Government's sacrosanct radio? Go, my dear, ask for your father's pardon. Why do you kick at the Goddess of Wealth that resides in your house?"

"Because I love you more than all the riches of the world, Radha!" I grew lyrical, eloquent, in the expression of my passion. "I will work as a teacher, as a clerk—I will do anything—but I will not go back to the house where I cannot keep you as my wife."

"Then do what you like, Babuji." There was a cold sting in that formal "Babuji" as if suddenly I had become a total stranger to her. In a voice that was colder than ice and sharper than the sharpest sword-blade, she said, "I have no desire to be the heroine of this Laila-Majnu drama." Finally, she dismissed me without even the pretence of politeness. "Go, Babuji, I have to get dressed. Soon it will be the hour of my business."

As I came down the stairs, the evening shadows had settled over the bazaar. A cool breeze was rustling through the tree-tops in the park. I felt a sudden shiver passing through my body. Now I remembered that I was wearing nothing over my silken shirt.

All this happened yesterday. Hardly 30 hours have passed since then. From Meerut to Delhi, I have travelled only 45 miles. But in these 30 hours and 45 miles, the world has changed for me. Yesterday, I was a careless rich young man, heir to a property worth a million. I was a well-known and even popular figure in my town. Fathers used to cite my shining example to their sons. Every mother was not only willing but eager to marry off her daughter to me. Several college girls made no secret of their romantic interest in me. And today I am a jobless, homeless vagrant on the streets, seeking shelter from the freezing cold wave behind a column in one of the curving arcades of Connaught Place. The stones under me are cold, I can't stop my teeth from chattering, and I have a fearful feeling that my mind is undergoing a slow process of paralysis.

Am I proud or obstinate? Am I suffering for an ideal or for a foolish, boyish whim? If I had gone back and fallen at my father's feet, surely he would have forgiven me. I would have been cosily wrapped up in my dressing gown, seated near the fireplace, sipping brandy. But more than the heat of the fireplace, I am in search of the warmth of love. More than my body, it is my soul that is shivering in the cold. My body is at least inadequately covered with an undervest and shirt, but in the last 30 hours my soul has been stripped of all the illusions which were its only protective coverings. Now it is stark naked in the "cold wave" that no meteorologist can ever predict or describe.

I did not want to remain in Meerut and cause a public scandal about leaving my home, and so I took a train to Delhi. I spent the night in a crowded Third Class waiting hall which looked—and stank—like a battlefield strewn with corpses. The stench from the toilet swept in with the draught every time someone went in or came out. And yet, after an hour of shivering in the train, the waiting hall was a heaven of refuge. Lying on a torn newspaper (which I had picked up from the dustbin) spread on the hard tiled floor, it was not easy to sleep. But I consoled myself—at least I am safe from the biting cold. Suddenly, it occurred to me that in such a big waiting hall, there was not even a fireplace or a heater. The pleasant warmth which I was now experiencing emanated from the mass of people sprawled there on the floor.

I somberly reflected that if I had been alone in that vast, draughty hall, I would have perished of exposure in the night and only my frozen corpse would have been discovered in the morning. Those 2 or 300 people—rough-hewn peasants from the villages, shrivelied-up clerks, hawkers, railway workers, beggars and mendicants—who lay there huddled against each other in all the contortions of their sleeping postures, had saved my life. But then, I too had contributed to each of them the warmth of my own body. Weren't we all involved in each other's survival? For a long time, I lay awake, pondering over the significance of that phenomenon, wondering what great truth lay hidden there in that mass of snoring humanity. Then a distant gong sounded the hour of five, a railway engine shunted along rattling the whole station building, and a railway babu shouted aloud, "Eh, you, get up, all of you, and clear out of the waiting hall. It's not your darling auntie's mansion!" And as a group of sweepers appeared with brooms and pails and mops, the sleepers woke and scrambled to get together their scattered belongings. I came out into the open where it was dark and cold, and the rows of street lamps were being switched off, one by one.

I went to call on several of my friends. Ram Dayal, who was my classmate and whose father owned a big cloth shop in Chandni Chowk, was very happy to see me and immediately suggested that we go to see a new film that was opening that day. But when I told him that I had left home and was looking for a job, all the warmth seemed to be drained out of his voice. "All right," he said quietly as if anxious to dismiss me before I could ask him for a loan, 'See me day after tomorrow. Today I'm rather busy. My father doesn't let me out of the shop for a second.'

"When I came out of his house and walked through Chandni Chowk, I saw that the sky was overcast with grey clouds and bare, autumn-stricken trees were trembling in the cold breeze blowing through the municipal park.

"Then I went to Amjad, whose father has a shoe factory. They were about to sit down to breakfast and insisted on my joining them. I did full justice to the *paranthas* dripping with *ghee*, spicy kebabs, dried fruit, carrot *halwa,* and had three cups of steaming tea. But when I explained to Amjad the circumstances in which I had left home and asked him to lend me a 100 rupees, he replied in a tone that was soft like ice-cream and just as cold. "So sorry, Baldeo, I'm rather hard up right now. Abba is very strict with cash, you know. But if you want two rupees…"

"I got up and as I walked through their garden, I saw that all the roses had wilted and withered in the cold winter night."

"From Old Delhi, I walked to New Delhi to Gurbachan Singh's bungalow. His father is Deputy Secretary in one of the Ministries. He was not in the same college with me but I had met him during a tennis tournament and together we had won the Men's Doubles. Since then, we were very good friends, calling each other "Partner". But he was not at home. His father told me that Gurbachan had gone to the club to play a game of tennis. So I trudged along to the club and found him in the card room playing rummy, "Hello, partner," he shouted as he saw me, "what will you have to drink?"

I declined the drink and called him out. When I told him the situation he said, "Sorry, old boy, but you know how hard it is to land a good job these days. I will seriously advise you to go back home. If you need the fare to Meerut I can lend it to you."

"No, thanks, Gurbachan," I said and walked out. He went back to the card room. As I came out of the club-gate, it began to drizzle. The ice cold drops of rain stung me through the shirt.

A cab driver hailed me. "Taxi, Babu Sahib?"

"Yes," I answered, trying to sound casual and nonchalant.

"Where to?"

"Meerut."

"So far! It will cost you ₹50."

"That's nothing. But it's Saturday and the banks close early today."

As I moved away, I heard the taxi driver telling someone behind my back, "I knew people go crazy in summer but this is the first one I have seen losing his head in a cold wave."

Then I went to the Employment Exchange. I went to several offices. I tried for a job in some shops. But there was no job for a young, healthy graduate. As the day dissolved into the shadows of the evening and the temperature fell steeply, one by one, all the illusions were peeled off my soul. Now it is past midnight; Connaught Place is desolate as the icy wind from Simla softly swishes through the arcades. They say in the papers that the cold wave is coming. I can feel it in my bones—it has arrived already. They say there will be an epidemic of influenza and cases of pneumonia. I feel a choking pain rising in my chest; I and my soul stand alone, naked, shivering in the desolation of the cold night. Is there such a thing as pneumonia of the soul? I wonder...

"*Babu*!" A rough-edged but thin voice broke upon the solitude of Baldeo's thoughts. He turned round and saw the outline of a woman, presumably a beggar, shivering in her rags, huddled behind the next column of the arcade.

"*Babu*, have you got maachis?"

Baldeo felt the useless matchbox in his pocket—the packet of cigarettes had long since been exhausted—and threw it to the woman behind the fat, round pillar.

The match was struck, a little flame leapt up in the murky darkness and the beggar woman's face glowed in the flickering circle of light. Pitch-black complexion. Layers of dust and dirt on the unwashed face. Unkempt matted hair. Baldeo shivered at the impact of her ugliness and thought of escaping from her neighborhood by seeking shelter in some other arcade.

The pin-point of fire at the glowing end of the *bidi* seemed to have imparted the warmth of life to the beggar woman. Baldeo saw that she was no longer shivering. Blowing out a thin streak of smoke, she said, "Father, O Father, how cold it is! Will you smoke a *bidi*, Babu?"

Baldeo wanted to refuse—he had no desire to strike up any kind of intimacy with the filthy woman in rags—but divining his hesitation, she added quickly, "It's only a matter of exchange. Babu, your *maachis*, my *bidi*. Take it."

She threw the packet of *bidis* at him and slid across the verandah floor to his side. "Here, light up your *bidi.*" A black callous hand brought the little flame to his lips. As the match lit up their faces, she was aghast to see the smooth-faced, silk-shirted "Babu". How could such a one have strayed out into her cold and ugly world? He, too, had a closer look at her face. Beneath the layers of dirt, the black face seemed to glow with a hidden fire like red-hot embers under a pile of ashes. The small and beady black eyes, too, had in them a flaming invitation. There was the yeast of youth in her bosom, and from her body rose a pungent odour which was compounded by dirt and sweat and poverty and youth and passion. They looked at each other for one brief, flickering moment till the match burnt out to the end, singing the woman's fingers. She dropped the match, and suddenly both of them were plunged in a pool of darkness. Baldeo felt the caress of a hot, quick breath on his face. The next moment, the match was struck again and Baldeo lit up his *bidi*.

Now they squatted in the verandah, reclining against their respective columns. Their *bidi*s were like two tiny stars in a dark, dark sky, beckoningly glowing at each other across the black vastness of the night.

As he puffed at his *bidi,* Baldeo felt his hand trembling. He touched his forehead. It was burning with fever. He inhaled a long, deep puff of smoke and a streak of pain slashed against his inside. Pneumonia ? He shivered with the cold premonition of death.

"Babu."

"Hoon?"

"Feel very cold—yes?"

No—but in that very instant, a sudden gust of wind sought him out and, piercing through his shirt, stabbed him in the heart with a dagger of ice.

"Babu, you are shivering with cold. Have you fever?"

"No, it is nothing." But as he said it, he could not stop his teeth from chattering.

"Babu, this cold is deadly. You may catch *namaoniya.*"

"Let it be!" he said, hoarsely, for now the noose of ice was choking and strangling him. His will, his consciousness, his very life was slowly, inexorably, helplessly, drifting towards an inevitable doom. With difficulty, he gasped out, "It's over now."

"No, Babu, no." In her voice was a cry of anguish, a plea for life, a challenge and invitation. "Come here, Babu. Come to me."

He forced his eyes open and saw the woman in the torn sari who was muffled in some rags.

"But you have no blanket, either."

"There is no blanket, *Babu*. But there is *me.*"

The fever burnt his brain. His breath was being choked out of him. He was no longer able to understand the subtlety of passion. But as a fierce cold blast crept down his spine, there was a tumultuous roar in his brain. Voices rang out across the horizon of his hallucination. Cold Wave! Cold Wave! Cold Wave!

Beware, beware! The Cold Wave is coming. In its wake will come influenza, pneumonia, death! Cold Wave! Cold Wave! Cold Wave! It was like the warning of doom, but soon it was drowned in a symphony of snoring in all the nasal notes of a million human beings huddled together in a vast, world-sized Third Class Waiting Hall. But in this new symphony, there was warmth, not freezing cold; there was the breath of life, not choking death. Baldeo felt himself sinking, sinking into the soft depths of a body saturated with the life-giving warmth of love. Now he was no longer afraid of the coldest cold wave!

SARDARJI

My name is Shaikh Burhanuddin.

When violence and murder became the order of the day in Delhi and the blood of Muslims flowed in the streets, I cursed my fate for having a Sikh for a neighbour. Far from expecting him to come to my rescue in times of trouble as a good neighbour should, I could not tell when he would thrust his *kirpan* into my belly. The truth is that till then, I used to find the Sikhs somewhat laughable. But I also disliked them and was somewhat scared of them.

My hatred for the Sikhs began on the day when I first set my eyes on one. I could not have been more than six years old when I saw a Sikh sitting out in the sun, combing his long hair. "Look," I yelled with revulsion, "a woman with a long beard!" As I got older, this dislike developed into hatred for the entire race.

It was a custom amongst old women of our household to heap all afflictions on our enemies. Thus, for example, if a child got pneumonia or broke its leg, they would say, "A long time ago, a Sikh (or an Englishman), got pneumonia; or a long time ago, a Sikh (or an Englishman) broke his leg." When I was older, I discovered that this referred to the year 1857 when the Sikh princes helped the *firangi*—foreigner—to defeat the Hindus and Muslims in the war of independence. I do not wish to propound a historical thesis but to explain the obsession, the suspicion and hatred which I bore towards the English and the Sikhs. I was more frightened of the English than of the Sikhs.

When I was 10 years old, I happened to be travelling from Delhi to Aligarh. I used to travel Third Class, or at the most in the Intermediate Class. That day I said to myself, "Let me for once travel Second Class and see what it feels like." I bought my ticket and found an empty Second Class compartment. I jumped on the well-sprung seats; I went into the bathroom and leapt up to see my face in the mirror; I switched on all the fans. I played with the light switches. There were only a couple of minutes for the train to leave when four red-faced Tommies burst into the compartment, mouthing obscenities: everything was either a "bloody" or a "damn". I had one look at them and my desire to travel Second Class vanished.

I picked up my suitcase and ran out. I only stopped for breath when I got into a Third Class compartment crammed with natives, But as luck would have it, it was full of Sikhs—their beards hanging down to their navels and dressed in nothing more than their underpants. I could not escape from them, but I kept my distance.

Although I feared the white man more than the Sikhs, I felt that he was more civilised; he wore the same kind of clothes as I. I also wanted to be able to say "damn", "bloody fool" the way he did. And like him, I wanted to belong to the ruling class. The Englishman ate his food with forks and knives; I also wanted to learn to eat with forks and knives so that natives would look upon me as advanced and as civilised as the white man.

My Sikh-phobia was of a different kind. I had contempt for the Sikh. I was amazed at the stupidity of men who imitated women and grew their hair long. I must confess I did not like my hair cut too short; despite my father's instructions to the contrary, I did not allow the barber to clip off more than a little when I went to him on Fridays. I grew a mop of hair so that when I played hockey or football, it would blow about in the breeze like those of English sportsmen. My father often asked me, "Why do you let your hair grow like a woman's?" My father had primitive ideas and I took no notice of his views. If he had had his way he would have had all heads razored bald, and stuck artificial beards on people's chins. That reminds me that the second reason for hating the Sikhs was their beards, which made them look like savages.

There are beards and beards. There was my father's beard, neatly trimmed in the French style, or my uncle's, which went into a sharp point under his chin. But what could you do with a beard to which no scissor was ever applied and which was allowed to grow like a wild bush—fed with a compost of oil, curd and goodness knows what. And, after it had grown a few feet, combed like hair on a woman's head: My grandfather also had a very long beard which he combed, but then my grandfather was my grandfather and a Sikh is just a Sikh.

After I had passed my matriculation examination, I was sent to the Muslim University at Aligarh. We boys who came from Delhi or the United Provinces looked down upon boys from the Punjab; they were crude rustics who did not know how to converse, how to behave at the table, or to deport themselves in polite company. All they could do was drink large tumblers of buttermilk. Delicacies such as vermicelli with essence of *kewra* sprinkled on it or the aroma of Lipton's tea was alien to them. Their language was unsophisticated to the extreme; whenever they spoke to each other it seemed as if they were quarrelling. It was full of *"assi, tussi, saadey, twhaaday"*. Heaven forbid, I kept my distance from the Punjabis.

But the warden of our hostel, (God forgive him), gave me a Punjabi as a room mate. When I realised that there was no escape, I decided to make the best of a bad bargain and be civil to the chap. After a few days, we became quite friendly. This man was called Ghulam Rasul and he was from Rawalpindi. He was full of amusing anecdotes and was a good companion.

You might well ask how Mr. Ghulam Rasul gate-crashed into a story about the Sikhs. The fact of the matter is that Ghulam Rasul's anecdotes were usually about the Sikhs. It is through these anecdotes that I got to know the racial characteristics, the habits and customs of this strange community. According to Ghulam Rasul, the chief characteristics of the Sikhs were the following:

All Sikhs were stupid and idiotic. At noon-time they lost their senses altogether. There were many instances to prove this. For example, one day at 12 o'clock, noon, a Sikh was cycling along Hall Bazaar in Amritsar when a constable, also a Sikh, stopped him and demanded, "Where is your light?" The cyclist replied nervously, *"Jemadar* Sahib, I lit it when I left my home; it must have gone out just now." The constable threatened to run him in.

A passer-by, yet another Sikh with a long, white beard, intervened: "Brothers, there is no point in quarrelling over little things. If the light has gone out, it can be lit again."

Ghulam Rasul knew hundreds of anecdotes of this kind. When he told them in his Punjabi accent, his audience was left helpless with laughter. One really enjoyed them best in Punjabi because the strange and incomprehensible behaviour of the uncouth Sikh was best told in his rustic lingo.

The Sikhs were not only stupid but incredibly filthy as well. Ghulam Rasul, who had known hundreds of them, told us how they never shaved their heads. And whereas we Muslims washed our hair thoroughly at least every Friday, the Sikhs, who made a public exhibition of bathing in their underpants, poured all kinds of filth, like curd, into their hair. I rub lime-juice and glycerine in my scalp. Although the glycerine is white and thick like curd, it is an altogether different thing—made by a well-known firm of perfumers of Europe. My glycerine came in a lovely bottle whereas the Sikh's curd came from the shop of a dirty sweetmeat seller.

I would not have concerned myself with the manner of living of these people except that they were so haughty and ill-bred as to consider themselves as good warriors as the Muslims. It is known over the world that one Muslim can get the better of 10 Hindus or Sikhs. But these Sikhs would not accept the superiority of the Muslim and would strut about like bantam cocks, twirling their moustaches and stroking their beards. Ghulam Rasul used to say that one day, we Muslims would teach the Sikhs a lesson that they would never forget.

Years went by.

I left college. I ceased to be a student and became a clerk; then a head clerk. I left Aligarh and came to live in New Delhi. I was allotted government quarters. I got married. I had children.

The quarters next to mine were occupied by a Sikh who had been displaced from Rawalpindi. Despite the passage of years, I remembered what Ghulam Rasul had told me. As Ghulam Rasul had prophesied, the Sikhs had been taught a bitter lesson in humility, at least in the district of Rawalpindi. The Muslims had virtually wiped them out. The Sikhs boasted that they were great heroes; they flaunted their long *kirpans*. But they could not withstand the brave Muslims. The Sikhs' beards were forcibly shaved. They were circumcised. They were converted to Islam. The Hindu press, as was its custom, vilified the Muslims. It reported that the Muslims had murdered Sikh women and children. This was wholly contrary to Islamic tradition. No Muslim warrior was ever known to raise his hand against a woman or a child. The pictures of the corpses of women and children published in Hindu newspapers were obviously fake. I wouldn't have put it beyond the Sikhs to murder their own women and children in order to vilify the Muslims.

The Muslims were also accused of abducting Hindu and Sikh women. The truth of the matter is that such was the impact of the heroism of Muslims on the minds of Hindu and Sikh girls that they fell in love with young Muslims and insisted on going with them. These noble-minded young men had no option but to give them shelter and thus bring them to the true path of Islam. The bubble of Sikh bravery was burst. It did not matter how their leaders threatened the Muslims with their *kirpans*, the sight of the Sikhs who had fled from Rawalpindi filled my heart with pride in the greatness of Islam.

The Sikh who was my neighbour was about 60 years old. His beard had gone completely grey. Although he had barely escaped from the jaws of death, he was always laughing, displaying his teeth in the most vulgar fashion. It was evident that he was quite stupid. In the beginning, he tried to draw me into his net by professions of friendship. Whenever I passed him he insisted on talking to me. I do not remember what kind of Sikh festival it was, when he sent me some sweet butter. My wife promptly gave it away to the sweepress. I did my best to have as little to do with him as I could. I snubbed him whenever I could. I knew that if I spoke a few words to him, he would be hard to shake off. Civil talk would encourage him to become familiar. It was known to me that Sikhs drew their sustenance from foul language. Why should I soil my lips by associating with such people?!

One Sunday afternoon, I was telling my wife of some anecdotes about the stupidity of the Sikhs. To prove my point, exactly at 12 o'clock, I sent my servant across to my Sikh neighbour to ask him the time. He sent back the reply, "two minutes after 12." I remarked to my wife, "You see, they are scared of even mentioning 12 o'clock!" We both had a hearty laugh. After this, many a time when I wanted to make an ass of my Sikh neighbour, I would ask him, "Well, Sardar*ji*, has it struck 12?" The shameless creature would grin baring all his teeth and answer, "Sir, for us it is always striking 12." He would roar with laughter as if it were a great joke.

I was concerned about the safety of my children. One could never trust a Sikh. And this man had fled from Rawalpindi. He was sure to have a grudge against Muslims and be on the lookout for an opportunity to avenge himself. I had told my wife never to allow the children to go near the Sikh quarters. But children are children. After a few days, I saw my children playing with the Sikh's little girl, Mohini, and his other grandchildren. This child, who was barely 10 years old, was really as beautiful as her name indicated; she was fair and beautifully formed. These wretches have beautiful women. I recall Ghulam Rasul telling me that if all the Sikh men were to leave their women behind and clear out of the Punjab, there would be no need for Muslims to go to paradise in search of *houris*.

The truth about the Sikhs was soon evident. After the thrashing in Rawalpindi, they fled like cowards to The East Punjab. Here, they found the Muslims weak and unprepared. So they began to kill them. Hundreds of thousands of Muslims were martyred; the blood of the faithful ran in streams. Thousands of women were stripped naked and made to parade through the streets. When Sikhs, fleeing from the West Punjab, came in large numbers to Delhi, it was evident that there would be trouble in the capital. I could not leave for Pakistan immediately. Consequently, I sent away my wife and children by air with my elder brother, and entrusted my own fate to God. I could not send much luggage by air. I booked an entire railway wagon to take my furniture and belongings. But on the day I was to load the wagon,

I got information that trains bound for Pakistan were being attacked by Sikh bands. Consequently, my luggage stayed in my quarters in Delhi.

On the 15th of August, India celebrated its independence. What interest could I have in the independence of India! I spent the day lying in bed, reading *Dawn* and the *Pakistan Times*. Both the papers had strong words to say about the manner in which India had gained its freedom and proved conclusively how the Hindus and the British had conspired to destroy the Muslims. It was only our leader, the great Mohammed Ali Jinnah, who was able to thwart their evil designs and win Pakistan for the Muslims. The English had knuckled under because of Hindu and Sikh pressure and handed over Amritsar to India. Amritsar, as the world knows, is a purely Muslim city. Its famous Golden Mosque—or am I mixing it up with the Golden Temple!—yes, of course, the Golden Mosque is in Delhi. And in Delhi besides the Golden Mosque there are the Jama Masjid, the Red Fort, the mausolea of Nizamuddin and Emperor Humayun, the tomb and school of Safdarjung—just everything worthwhile bears imprints of Islamic rule. Even so, this Delhi (which should really be called after its Muslim builder Shahjahan, as Shahjahanabad) was to suffer the indignity of having the flag of Hindu imperialism unfurled on its ramparts.

My heart seemed rent asunder. I could have shed tears of blood. My cup of sorrow was full to the brim when I realised that Delhi, which was once the footstool of the Muslim Empire, the centre of Islamic culture and civilisation, had been snatched out of our hands. Instead, we were to have the desert wastes of the West

Punjab, Sindh and Baluchistan inhabited by an uncouth and uncultured people. We were to go to a land where people do not know how to talk in civilised Urdu; where men wear baggy *salwars* like their women folk; where they eat thick bread four pounds in weight instead of the delicate wafers we eat at home!

I steeled myself. I would have to make this sacrifice for my great leader, Jinnah, and for my new country, Pakistan. Nevertheless, the thought of having to leave Delhi was most depressing.

When I emerged from my room in the evening, my Sikh neighbour bared his fangs and asked, "Brother, did you not go out to see the celebrations?" I felt like setting fire to his beard.

One morning, the news spread of a general massacre in Old Delhi. Muslim homes were burnt in Karol Bagh. Muslim shops in Chandni Chowk were looted. This, then, was a sample of Hindu rule! I said to myself, "New Delhi is really an English city; Lord Mountbatten lives here as well, as the Commander-in-Chief. At least in New Delhi no hand will be raised against Muslims." With this self assurance, I started towards my office. I had to settle the business of my provident fund; I had delayed going to Pakistan in order to do so. I had only got as far as Gole Market when I ran into a Hindu colleague in the office. He said, "What on earth are you up to? Go back at once and do not come out of your house. The rioters are killing Muslims in Connaught circus."

I hurried back home.

I had barely got to my quarters when I ran into my Sikh neighbour. He began to reassure me. "Shaikh*ji*, do not worry! As long as I am alive, no one will raise a hand against you." I said to myself: "How much fraud is hidden behind this man's beard! He is obviously pleased that the Muslims are being massacred, but expresses sympathy to win my confidence; or is he trying to taunt me?" I was the only Muslim living in the block, perhaps I was the only one on the road.

I did not want these people's kindness or sympathy. I went inside my quarter and said to myself, "If I have to die, I will kill at least 10 or 20 men before they get me." I went to my room where, beneath my bed, I kept my double-barrelled gun. I had also collected quite a hoard of cartridges. I searched the house, but could not find the gun.

"What is *huzoor* looking for?" asked my faithful servant, Mohammed.

"What happened to my gun?"

He did not answer. But I could tell from the way he looked that he had either hidden it or stolen it.

"Why don't you answer?" I asked him angrily.

Then he came out with the truth. He had stolen my gun and given it to some of his friends who were collecting arms to defend the Muslims in Daryaganj.

"We have hundreds of guns, several machine guns, 10 revolvers and a cannon. We will slaughter these infidels; we will roast them alive."

"No doubt with my gun you will roast the infidels in Daryaganj, but who will defend me here? I am the only Mussulman amongst these savages. If I am murdered, who will answer for it?"

I persuaded him to steal his way to Daryaganj to bring back my gun and a couple of hundred cartridges.

When he left, I was convinced that I would never see him again. I was all alone. On the mantlepiece was a family photograph My wife and children stared silently at me. My eyes filled with the tears at the thought that I would never see them again. I was comforted with the thought that they were safe in Pakistan. Why had I been tempted by my paltry provident fund and not gone with them? I heard the crowd yelling.

"Sat Sri Akal."

"Har Har Mahadev."

The yelling came closer and closer. They were rioters—the bearers of my death warrant. I was like a wounded deer running hither and thither, with the hunters' hounds in full pursuit. There was no escape. The door was made of very thin wood and glass panes. The rioters would smash their way in.

"Sat Sri Akal."

"Har Har Mahadev."

They were coming closer and closer; death was coming closer and closer. Suddenly, there was a knock at the door. My Sikh neighbour walked in, "Shaikh*ji*, come into my quarters at once." Without a second thought, I ran into the Sikh's verandah and hid behind the columns. A shot hit the wall above my head. A truck drew up and about a dozen young men climbed down. Their leader had a list in his hand—Quarter No. 8—Shaikh Burhanuddin. He read my name and ordered his gang to go ahead. They invaded my quarter and under my very eyes proceeded to destroy my home. My furniture, boxes, pictures, books, druggets and carpets, even the dirty linen was carried into the truck. Robbers! Thugs! Cut-throats!

As for the Sikh, who had pretended to sympathise with me, he was no less a robber than they! He was pleading with the rioteers: "Gentlemen, stop! We have prior claim over our neighbour's property. We must get our share of the loot." He beckoned to his sons and daughters. All of them gathered to pick up whatever they could lay their hands on. One took my trousers; another a suitcase.

They even grabbed the family photograph. They took the loot to their quarters.

You bloody Sikh! If God grants me life, I will settle my score with you. At this moment I cannot even protest. The rioteers are armed and only a few yards away from me. If they get to know of my presence...

"Please come in."

My eyes fell on the unsheathed *kirpan* in the hands of the Sikh. He was inviting me to come in. The bearded monster looked more frightful after he had soiled his hands with my property. There was the glittering blade of his *kirpan* inviting me to my doom. There was no time to argue. The only choice was between the guns of the rioteers and the sabre of the Sikh. I decided, rather the *kirpan* of the old man than 10 armed gangsters. I went into the room hesitantly, silently.

"Not here, come in further." I went into the inner room like a goat following a butcher. The glint of the blade of the *kirpan* was almost blinding.

"There you are, take your things," said the Sikh.

He and his children put all the stuff they had pretended to loot in front of me. His old woman said, "Son, I am sorry we were not able to save more."

I was dumbfounded.

The gangsters had dragged out my steel almirah and were trying to smash it open. "It would be simpler if we could find the keys," said someone.

"The keys can only be found in Pakistan. That cowardly son of a filthy Muslim has decamped," replied another.

Little Mohini answered back: "Shaikh*ji* is not a coward. He had not run off to Pakistan."

"Where is he blackening his face?"

"Why should he be blackening his face? He is in..." Mohini realised her mistake and stopped in her sentence. Blood mounted in her father's face. He locked me in the inside room, gave his *kirpan* to his son and went out to face the mob.

I do not know what exactly took place outside. I heard the sound of blows; then Mohini crying; then the Sikh yelling full-blooded abuse in Punjabi. And then a shot and the Sikh's cry of pain: *"Hai."*

I heard a truck engine starting up; and then there was a petrified silence.

When I was taken out of my prison, my Sikh neighbour was lying on a charpoy. Beside him lay a torn and blood-stained shirt. His new shirt also was oozing with blood. His son had gone to telephone for the doctor.

"Sardar*ji*, what have you done?" I do not know how these words came out of my lips. The world of hate in which I had lived all these years, lay in ruins about me.

"Sardar*ji*, why did you do this?" I asked him again.

"Son, I had a debt to pay."

"What kind of a debt?"

"In Rawalpindi there was a Muslim like you who sacrificed his life to save mine and the honour of my family."

"What was his name, Sardarji?"

"Ghulam Rasul."

Fate had played a cruel trick on me. The clock on the wall started to strike...1...2...3...4...5... The Sikh turned towards the clock and smiled. He reminded me of my grandfather with his 12-inch beard. How closely the two resembled each other!

...6...7...8...9... We counted in silence.

He smiled again. His white beard and long white hair were like a halo, effulgent with a divine light...10...11...12... The clock stopped striking.

I could almost hear him say, "For us Sikhs, it is always 12 o'clock!" But the bearded lips, still smiling, were silent. And I knew he was already in some distant world, where the striking of clocks counted for nothing, where violence and mockery were powerless to hurt him.

Translated by Khushwant Singh

LETAR FROM A CHILD TO MAHATMA GANDHI

To
Mahatama Gandhi Sahib,
c/o Gaud Olmaity
Haven

Bapu!
I am not myself alone riting this letar but others are making me rite it. Those who are making me rite are as falous: My yunger brother Bundoo (whose real name is Banday Ali), my elder sister Zenab and yunger sister Sakina, our naybours son Gopal and Gopal's yunger sister Seeta. And, yes, Mohun, a little refooji boy from Panjab who lives near us. I almost had forgot him. You see he aulso wants me to rite to you but he has sed it not with his tung, but with his eyes. He does not say anything with his tung. He speeks only throo his eyes. His eyes speek much but I will tell you about them after. At this time I only want to say that Mohuns eyes are also saying rite to Bapu. So I am riting this letar. Please axkuse me. Wont you Bapu.

You are a grate man. You must be thinking why the childs riting letar to me. But we hear you like childs very much. In one foto I saw you sitting and lafing with childs. Gopal says he saw you one time on Juhu beech playing with little childs just like them. And Mohun when he seez your foto his eyes wich are always so sad looking become brite with happiness and say he is our bapu why should we fear him. If you will axkuse me I will say that in your lafing foto you luk just like child or baby who has no teeth even like Gopals smol brother who also drinks goats milk just like you.

My name is Anwar Ali. But every one calls Annu. My fathers name is Akbar Ali. I am eight year old. My mothers name is Fatma but everyone calls her Fatto (no she is not fat but fatto is smol for Fatma). Her mother also lives with us. Grandmother is very very old all white hair and not teeth. (Just like you). This our hole family except my sisters Zainab and Sakina.

My father did not like you. He sed Gandhi is enemy of Muslims. Mother sed what father sed. But Grandmother she says Gandhi is Gaud's man and he see everyone like brother. Father says Grandmother is too old so cannot understand difficult work of politiks. Father is much ejukated at Aligarh collij and read paper every day so we believed him not Grandmother. So when talk was about you we sed bad things about you and lafed also bekos you luked so funy with your naked bady and loin-clothes.

One day we heard India was to be cut in two pieces like Grandfathers property after his death half come to father and half went to uncle. One day I asked Father what is Pakistan. He said it will be country of Muslims own, where we will have our own raj. I was very hapy to hear this bekos in a paper of colour fotos I once saw foto of one raja all in gold and silver cloths and waring daimands and perls in nek. So I sed when we Muslims have our own raj we will all bekum rajas ans were gold and silver cloths and daimonds and perls in our neks. And we shouted Pakistan Zindabad, Pakistan Zindabad!

Then after Pakistan was made we herd Hindus beating Muslims every were. That is what my father who reads paper sed. So we were angry and hated Hindus. But one thing I did not understand. Muslims were many in sum places like Panjab Fruntier Sind—why they not beating and killing Hindus who were few. Perhaps they were doing it olrite but Father sed no only Hindus bad and making trouble for Muslims. After ol I am child. So I kept quait and sed nothing befor Father but in my hart I thout much.

Now I want to tel you about my gun. It is very beyutiful and nise and makes big nois. My father gave it me on my fifth birthday saying I must play with gun and bekum soljar of Pakistan. It is reely only playing air gun but all childs fear it and with it I paraid my Pakistani Fauj of childs which contens my sisters and brother.

In house next to us is Hindu Sena of Gopal. Oll childs is like us. Gopals Father is rich baniya merchant like oll Hindus that is what father says. Gopals unkel very strong Hindu and paraids in Shwaji Park with Hindu Sangh army. They oll hate Muslims and Gopal paraids his Hindu Sena everyday. But they have no gun like mine only tin pistel and bow and arros of bamboo. They shouts Har Har Mahadev and Hindu raj banaengay. They also shouts other Hindy crys. They are ten twelve childs and we only four childs but we not afred. We brave Muslims and we have gun after oll. We fite them when they come. When they shouts Har Har Mahadev we shouts more Allah O Akbar. When they shouts Hindu Raj, Hindu Raj we shouts Pakistan Zindabad. We live in Shwaji Park with Hindus olround. Father says we not to shout like that or Hindus will kill us. Grandmother also tells us not to but we not afred. One day Gopals army attack us so we fite and they run away when I sho them gun. But Bundoo fall down fearing Gopals pistel.

When we were fiting I saw Mohan for fust time. He was sitting on boundri woll luking at our fite with stranje eyes like he had seen much fite befor and not like it. When I went near him I saw he was crying with tears but not speaking only luking with stranje eyes. I once saw a mad fakir his eyes were just like this. So I thout this also some mad child or may be dumb so cannot speak. Then Gopal came and sed don't teese Mohan he pore refooji boy from Panjab whose father killed and so he now staying with relashuns. I felt very sory and did not injoy playing with gun. At nite I saw in bad dreems Mohans stranje eyes luking at me and I cried in sleep and mother sed there there, take name of Allah seven times and devils will not truble you. I took name of Allah seven times but devils trubled me oll nite.

Mohan alwez sat on boundri woll and saw our play with those stranje mad eyes. He played not with us nor with Gopal only sat quait thinking Gaud nows what. And madness increased in his eyes and we wondered what they had seen that he bekum like that.

We herd on radio you were fasting unless Hindus of Delhi bekum olrite with Muslims. When she herd it teers came in Grandmothers eyes and she did not eat for one hole day and even Father sed if there is one good man in Hindus he is Gandhi. Trying to copy Grandmother I also fasted one time but befor evening I was in bad condishun and my hart was not in play or school work but only in fud and oll time I think of pulao and shami kababs. And I thout how you can fast for such long time and not eat anything.

When you were fasting for many days and we herd in hole country Hindus Muslims were saying they were sory for beating and killing each other and swaring befor you they will not fite now we also stoped play of Hindu Sena and Pakistani Fauj.

At play time we all sitting quait and not playing when Gopal comes and says Hello Annu.

I sed hello Gopal what is the talk.

He sed Bapuji and started crying with teers.

That day radio sed you were very week and sick and cannot speek even, so thinking of that I also began weeping.

Gopal luked at me with surprise and asked you also crying?

I sed yes after oll he is doing oll this for Muslims.

Gopal thout and sed from today no more play of Hindu Muslim fite.

I sed yes when oll stoping fite we also must stop. When oll caching ears and swaring not to fite we also cach our ears.

Then we deside we wil brake gun pistel bows arrows everything and thro in see.

And when I luk at Mohan the pore refooji boy for fust time I see small hapines in his eyes and I think it is like majik.

Next day Father also sed Gandhiji done majik to Delhi and oll Hindus and Muslims and Sikhs caching there ears and swaring not to fite and Muslims getting their mosks and everything olrite in Delhi. So we are hapy to here you brok your fast and also go to tomb of Muslim saint Khaja Qutbuddin at time of Urs.

I and Gopal yesterday had agree to brake gun and pistel atsetra but now when I see gun oll shiny and brite I don't like braking it and throing in see. Also I think Gopal not brake his pistel why not I also keep gun. I is not using it after oll only keeping it for sum rite moment.

Gopal also thout same suppose Annu not brake gun why I loos my pistel.

After you broke fast we felt beter. Sumhow when we herd you sick and week, hart was trubled like Father or Mother be sick. Not only I and Gopal but oll people. Now I know why oll call you Bapu.

Then one morning we here bad news sumone throo bomb on you. Thank Gaud you were olrite and man who thro bomb arrested.

I say to Gopal—Gopal this is very bad. Bad people want to kill Gandhiji.

Gopal says yes we must gard Gandhijis life.

I sed how.

He sed we will go to Delhi and stand like soljers to gard Gandhijis house.

I sed suppose sum bad people come what you can do without gun or sord. …

He spoke in hury why I have pistel and bows and arros. Then he bekum quait at once like he spok by mistaik.

I also spok in hury without thinking. What is pistel. I will gard with my gun.

Gopal luked at me and sed were you got gun from.

I also speek like that, from were you got pistel and arros.

He sed angrily you Muslims are like that no one can beleev you. You promised to brake gun.

Why shud I remane quait. I also speek angrily you Hindus tell lies. You promised to brake pistel.

Go I don't want to play with you. I sed and came home and tuk out gun cleaned it and put oil in its mashinry. I must prepare for fite with Hindu Sena.

In their hous Gopal and his brother also sit and prepare their pistel and arros and bows.

Next time I see Mohan the pore refooji boy I see sem old feer in his eyes.

Days passed. One evening we are paying on see beech in frunt of our house when Father comes rushing from offis and says Gandhiji ded, killed by some mad man.

Fust no one beleev but radio also say Gandhiji ded so hav to beleev. Then I thought see no one gard him proper. How man with pistel go nere him. I wish I and Gopal not quareld and gone to gard Gandhiji. At Delhhi.

That nite no one eat oll sitting near radio. We herd Pandit Jawaharlal Nehru. He is so grate man but weeping like childs. Speeking and weeping oll time. so I also cry with teers. Every one cry. Even teers in eyes of father.

I kud not sleep proper. I saw in bad dreems bad man coming to kill you and I crying shouting save Gandhiji his life in danjer but no one listen. Most bad dreem I saw bad man shuting you with my gun. And I thout that is why you bekum angry with me and go away to haven.

It was hurtal next day and eskool klosed. But our hart not in play. On boundri woll I see Mohan and he crying. Seeing him I also cry agen. Gopal comes he also crying.

Gopal sed Bapuji is gon.

I sed yes Grandmother says Allah has kalled him to haven.

Then Gopal says I saw him in dreem.

My hart fills with feer so I say. You saw in dreem the sum one killing with my gun.

No no, Gopal says crying, I see in dreem sum one killing Bapu with my pistel...

I tell him about my dreem. Gopal says Bapu angry with us both so gon away to haven. Then oll of us cry and don't know what to do.

p.s.

February 13,

I rote this letar many days befor but not put in post thinking I forgoten to rite sumthing important. Now I rite it.

Yesterday your ashes wer put in meny rivers and sees. On chopati we see with our own eyes. Very many people in proseshun also meny Muslims oll crying with teers.

You will be glad to heer our gorement cach many bad people who want kill you and make Hindus Muslims fite. And in Pakistan Hindustan oll Hindus Muslims caching their eers and swaring never fite again. Now you excuse them and come back.

Yesterday evening after oll people go away I vent to see beech and brake my gun and thro it in wotar. There I see Gopals pistel and arros and bow lying broken in wotar.

So now oll of us myself Gopal Bundoo Zenab Sakina Seeta oll cach eers and sware we will never fite agen. Please axkuse us and kum back.

You will kum back, wont you, Bapu?

TWELVE HOURS

It was a cold December night!

The clock in the Station Master's office showed a quarter to seven. "Another 15 minutes for the train," thought Bina and resumed pacing up and down the platform.

It was a small station with neither a bookstall nor a restaurant. It was not possible to get even a cup of tea. The station building was a two-room affair. One displayed a board, "Station Master", the other was the booking office. There was no one at the booking window. Two peasants, huddled up in their coarse blankets and with the ends of their turbans wrapped round their ears to keep out the chilly breeze, sat like formless ghosts in a corner of the verandah. Far in the distance, the red light of the signal shone out of the darkness.

Bina was wearing a woollen sweater. Over it was a shawl. But at the moment, she did not need them for she was not feeling cold. Since she had joined the Revolutionary Party, it was the first occasion on which an important piece of work had been entrusted to her. The thought of this quickened her heartbeat and her cheeks felt feverish despite the icy breeze. Would she be able to do what she had been told? Or would she get nervous?

Would she fail the Party? She was prepared to face any danger for the cause. She did not care even if it involved a risk to her life. And then, the present assignment was simple enough. The instructions that the Secretary had given were echoing in her ears.

"Look here, our old comrade, Vijay Singh, is returning home after 16 years in prison. But we have learnt that as soon as he reaches the city, he will be arrested again because the police fear that his return will further enhance the prestige and strength of the Revolutionary Party. So we have asked him to get off the train at Ramnagar. You must meet him at the station. He will spend the night at your house. In the morning, he can go to the city and let the police arrest him. But we want him to be free for at least 12 hours." The Secretary had seemed to emphasise that—"Twelve hours! A man deserves that after 16 years of living hell." Then he had given her a sealed letter. "Give it to him and deliver his reply at the Party office the very next day. He will spend the night at your house!"

But Bina's house consisted of just two small rooms. A schoolteacher earning Rs 60 a month could afford nothing better! Besides, she lived alone. No family, no relations—not even a servant. She cooked her own food. Under these circumstances, would it be quite right for a stranger to spend the night under the same roof?

Bina had been born and brought up in a conventional "respectable" household. A college education had no doubt freed her mind to a great extent but the fear of society, of public opinion, still lurked in her subconscious. What would people say? This fear gnawed at her heart. But she also felt the indescribable attraction of male company, the secret unspoken and suppressed desire for the experience she had so far denied herself. Desire and fear! Fear and desire! She was young and physically awakened, but completely inexperienced in the ways of love. With the help of her book-knowledge, she could participate in an academic discussion on the principles of sex, but was ignorant of its practical implications. And yet, Nature had created a certain tension in her body, a sensation that was at once ticklish and soothing, delicious stabs of pain, a strange fever. She knew there was only one cure for this malady. But to take a dose of the medicine before marriage—that was out of the question!

Far in the dark distance, the red light suddenly turned green. The railway lines, dully glistening in the half-light of the solitary lamp on the platform, were beginning to echo the distant thunder of the incoming train. Bina's attention was diverted from the eternal problems of sex to the strange personality of the man who was arriving by that train and who would be her guest for the next 12 hours. Vijay Singh! It was a name to reckon with in the annals of revolution. His revolutionary achievements were still remembered. Today, he was coming back after spending 16 years in prison. Tomorrow he might be locked up again. Such was his life. He was afraid neither of jails nor of the gallows. She had seen his picture in the Party office—a handsome, strong, broad-shouldered young man with a noble forehead and bright black eyes which, even in a picture, seemed to hypnotise. Beautiful eyes. Terrible eyes. There was passion, madness in their depths, but on the surface was childish simplicity. It was impossible to look at those eyes and not be fascinated. Bina had learnt from these eyes her first revolutionary lesson. She had learnt from them the passion for freedom, the utter devotion to the cause, the determination to sacrifice everything for it. Everything. Money. Position. Family. Material comforts. Life. Even honour! Whenever she felt unsteady on the perilous paths of revolution, she looked at those eyes, and in a moment, her whole being was filled with a strange power and then she felt she could face any difficulty, make any sacrifice.

But those eyes were not merely the eyes of a revolutionary. They were also the eyes of man. There was in them a wild, animal attraction. A flame of passion. An invitation to taste the forbidden fruit. A glimpse of that fascinating world, the door of which was barred by society to unmarried girls like Bina. But she knew this door could be broken open. She knew many girls in the Party who had broken it down and stepped into the world of free love in open defiance to society. Could she too do it—tonight? The very thought brought a blush to her cheeks. She ought not to think of such things. It was disgraceful that she, Bina, who had dedicated her life to the cause of Revolution, should be thinking such evil thoughts. But were they really evil thoughts? And if they were evil, could she really keep them out of her mind? She knew she could not.

The train came alongside the platform and stopped. Bina's mind was jerked back to reality. It was a three-minute stop and few passengers cared even to look out of the train windows. She ran from one end of the platform to the other but could find no one even faintly resembling the picture in the Party office. The solitary passenger who got down from the train was a bearded old man in shabby clothes, perhaps a beggar. The two peasants got up from their corner in the verandah and were soon swallowed up by the mass of humanity jammed into a Third Class compartment. The engine gave a whistle and the train, puffing wearily, was on its way. Had Vijay Singh, then, missed the train? Or had he been arrested already? And why was that old man, standing under the light, looking at her so closely?

"Are you Miss Bina?" There was a note of refinement in the old man's voice.

And as she said "Yes", she saw his eyes—eyes that were shining out of the bushy growth of unkempt hair like two lighted windows of a house in a thick jungle.

"You ... you ... you are Comrade Vijay Singh?"

"Yes. I got a message from the Party Secretary that I was to get down here and that you would come to meet me."

"Let's go."

Bina brought Vijay Singh home. She had prepared some food before she had gone to the station and immediately served it in a gleaming brass *thali*. Without a word, he started eating. He did not even formally ask, "Won't you eat too?"

She sat down on a chair by his side. Vijay Singh was eating silently, hungrily, greedily—as if he had not eaten for days. Tears of compassion filled Bina's eyes when she realised that after 16 years of the horrible jail diet, this was the first real meal he was having. She looked at him intently. Was this the same handsome, broad-shouldered

Vijay Singh whose picture hung in the Party office? No, he could not be the same person! How could he be? His head was almost bald with ugly sores caused by infectious water or the lack of washing facilities in jail. His beard—half black and half white—grew in a most frightening manner. The hair above and below his lips had become discoloured yellow, his teeth looked pyorrheatic. In spite of the deep compassion and admiration she felt for him, Bina shuddered at the thought that a few seconds before the train arrived, she had been imagining an amorous adventure with this very man!

When Vijay Singh had finished eating, the *thali* empty and swept clean, Bina said "Would you like a bath now? Here are the clothes the Party has sent for you. I am putting some hot water in the bathroom for you." As she said this, Vijay Singh cast a look on the rags he was wearing, as though he had suddenly become conscious of his dirty appearance. Without a word, he went to the bathroom. He had spent many years out of the 16 in solitary confinement and it seemed he had lost the habit of talking to people. In Bina's presence, he was particularly silent, as if he were utterly dumb!

He emerged from the bathroom, looking somewhat cleaner and less tired. He sat down by the coal-stove which Bina had lighted because of the cold and in the red glow of the burning coals, Bina saw a gleam of happiness in his eyes—as if the ashes had been shaken off the embers! He borrowed Bina's scissors and cut his long, dirty nails. Then he asked for the Party Secretary's letter and settled down to read it. Bina knew that it contained an exhaustive review of the political situation for the last 16 years and a report of the Party's work. As he read it, the old revolutionary fire returned to his eyes. Anger. Sorrow. Happiness. One could see the succeeding emotions in his eyes. After he had read the report, he was once again a leader of the Revolutionary Party. He had to give his suggestions and instructions to the Party before he was sent back to the prison. He asked Bina for pen and paper and sat down to write. But she noticed that his rough, bony hand shook as he wrote. After 16 years of turning the handmill, his fingers had lost their suppleness.

When he finished the letter, he gave it to Bina and asked her to deliver it to the Secretary. Bina looked at the watch. It was only quarter past nine. To break the silence, she said, "Do you want to sleep now or would you like to sit up a little longer?"

The reply she received surprised her. "I want to go to a cinema—a talking cinema." In a flash, her mind saw the grim reality of prison life. Sixteen years! From 1927 to 1943! So Vijay had never been to a talkie. He had neither heard Saigal's melodies nor seen Joan Fontaine's beautiful acting. To him, names like Paul Muni and Bette Davis and Kananbala and Ashok Kumar would mean nothing. He was as ignorant of the magic of the talking pictures as a man living in the darkest interiors of Africa. For 16 years, he had been denied the beauties and pleasures of life. Cinema and theatre. Song and dance. Women's voices and children's laughter. The pageantry of the sunset. Flowers in spring. The shade of trees and the velvet of green grass. Love. The love of a mother. The love of children. A woman's love. Nothing. Nothing. Only a dirty dark cell. The harsh brutal voices of wardens and prison officials. The company of hardened criminals and murderers. An island of death in the ocean of life, beyond the frontier of humanity. And there he had spent 16 years. One hundred and ninety two months—nearly 6000 days of anguish and 6000 nights of despair. After all that he had suffered, he had been granted only 12 hours of freedom. Twelve hours of life. Twelve hours of light and colour and laughter. And then again, the huge doors of prison would swallow him.

"I want to go to a cinema—a talking cinema." With childish naivety he had made this request. There is a child in every man. And even a revolutionary is human after all. Why should it be surprising that he had this strong desire to go to a cinema? Who knew, he might never come out alive from the prison. He might go to his death with this one desire unfulfilled!

There was only one cinema in the little town of Ramnagar where outdated Indian films were shown. Bina had never been there before; she now took Vijay Singh with her. The show was about to start and by the time they entered, the lights were switched off. Pictures began to move and speak on the screen. The film was *Toofan Mail*. An old cheap and crude film. But for Vijay Singh, it was no less than a miracle. Years ago, before his arrest, he had seen moving pictures, but to hear them talk and even sing absolutely astounded him. He laughed like an uninhibited child at the antics of Charlie and Ghory. When the other spectators began to look back, Bina felt terribly embarrassed. But the next moment, she remembered that Vijay Singh was laughing like this perhaps for the first time in 16 years and she too began to enjoy the picture which she had seen before and thoroughly disliked.

On the screen, Madhuri and Billimoria were playing the game of love—love that was carefree, sensuous and full of gay abandon. Not the love that expresses itself in sighs and tears of frustration but the love that is echoed in ringing laughter and shines out of suggestive glances. Madhuri, in a tight dress that clung to the contours of her body, was desire personified.

Vijay Singh was engrossed in watching the film. But his hand—had he let it touch Bina's by mistake? It was hard and coarsened by manual labour but still there was a certain warmth about it. Once it must have been a delicate and sensitive hand. The fingers were still long and tapering. Vijay Singh was watching the play of shadows on the screen and his hand was placed on Bina's. But he was not making any attempt to increase the pressure of the contact. Bina thought, "He must have touched my hand by mistake," and she gently withdrew hers. It was dark in the hall. Yet Bina felt as if Vijay Singh resented her taking away the hand. After that, his interest in the film manifestly grew less. A little later, he said, "Let's go home. I have seen enough." And when they came out in the light of the street lamps, Bina found him walking, like a sulky child, with his eyes fixed on the road.

When they reached home, Bina made a bed for Vijay Singh on her own cot. Then she spread her own bedding on the floor in the other room. Placing a glass of water on the table, she asked him, "Do you want anything else?" and he shook his head to say, "No". But Bina saw that his eyes were fixed on her face. In their depths was the same gleam of passion, on their surface was the same child-like simplicity and that animal magnetism, too, that she had felt in the picture in the Party office. Presently, the eyes grew dim and misty and in them, Bina saw an appeal instead of desire. Quickly she switched off the light and went to her own room.

But the latch was on the other side of the door—on Vijay Singh's side! As she closed the door, she said, "Please put the latch on." She thought, "Is he already asleep?" But from the other room came the sound of the creaking cot. He was turning over. After a while, it seemed he had got up from the bed. He was not asleep. He was walking about in the room.

Bina knew the reason for his restlessness. After 16 years of a lonely, loveless life, the love scene in *Toofan Mail* had aroused his dormant passions. Tomorrow morning he would go back to jail. There were just a few hours left.

For so long, Bina had deprived herself of sensuous pleasures. Was she to offer her virgin body now to satisfy the passions of an ugly, diseased old man? She had always dreamt of a healthy, handsome young man who would love her and whom she could love, whom she would marry and from whom she would have children. She waited for him to come into her life and was still waiting. What a fall from that ideal to this reality—to this wreck of a human being! No, she could never do it!

But her sensitive and sympathetic mind presented the other side of the same situation. True, Vijay Singh is prematurely old. There is a frightening growth of beard in his face. There are wrinkles on his forehead and sores on his bald head. But why? Think Bina, think! Sixteen years ago, this very Vijay Singh was young and handsome and healthy. You have seen his picture, haven't you? Can you swear you never looked at it with the eyes of desire? Today, why is that same Vijay Singh in this miserable state? Why? A young man of 25 cannot grow so old and decrepit in 16 years. Why did Vijay Singh lose his youth, his health, his looks? For the Revolution, Bina, for the Revolution! The same Revolution for which you are willing to sacrifice your life. But you only talk; he has shown what he can do! He sacrificed the best years of his youth, his romantic dreams, his friends and relations, everything. He suffered whippings, the kicks and abuses of the wardens, he has passed months in solitary confinement, like an animal in a cage. Why? For the Revolution! And you, you are so heartless and selfish that you look with disgust at his beard, his wrinkles and his sores. Shame on you, woman!

In the other room, Vijay Singh was still walking about. His footsteps came up to the door and then stopped. Bina's heart almost stopped beating. There was neither the sound of the latch being put on nor was the door opened. After a few seconds, the footsteps retreated; Bina's heart began to beat again.

No, he will never take the initiative. He is sensitive. He knows he is ugly and unattractive. He will not dare to approach you. If you don't go into that room, he will spend the whole night pacing up and down the room and in the morning, he will go back to jail without a word. The man who had passed 16 years without love can also pass the rest of his life like that. But if you allow him to go back disappointed, you will never forgive yourself. His eyes, full of pitiful desire and yearning, will always haunt you.

Vijay Singh's restless footsteps stopped. She heard the bed creak. He had laid himself down again.

"Maybe he will sleep," Bina tried to console herself. But immediately, she heard him turning over on the bed. And what was that? Were her ears deceiving her or was he really crying? Vijay Singh, of whom it was said that he laughed when they whipped him! Vijay Singh, who had smiled even on receiving the death sentence! The same Vijay Singh who had been on hunger-strike for 50 days, who was afraid neither of death nor of deportation! The same Vijay Singh was crying today, sobbing like a child.

Vijay Singh's eyes had failed to awaken desire in Bina's heart. He had touched her hand and it had meant nothing to her. But hearing him cry, something snapped within her. Crying children have to be petted and comforted and given something to keep them quiet. And wasn't the great revolutionary, Vijay Singh, also a child in this respect—in spite of his beard, his wrinkles and sores!

From the depths of her being, conventional morality raised its head and tried to argue with her: "Don't forget that honour is a woman's most cherished treasure. How can you squander it like this?" And when she was not convinced, it tried to frighten her: "He is sick. He has sores on his body. You might catch some infection."

But at that moment, Bina was thinking of those horrible 16 years which Vijay Singh had passed in jail—that long period in which every pleasure of life had been denied to him. Cinema and theatre, song and dance, the laughter of children and women's voices.

And tomorrow, these 12 hours of life would have passed and he would be consigned to that same hell again. Vijay

Singh would go back with his desire being unsatisfied. He had given his whole life to the cause of his country. But for him, a woman could not give up her body even for a few hours. A woman's love. Softness and warmth. A throbbing heart next to one's own. These things had been lost to him for 16 years, and if he did not get them now, he might never get them before his death.

No, she would not let that happen. She had dedicated her life to the Revolution. Her life. Her body. Her honour. What was the value of her miserable body when compared to the sacrifices Vijay Singh had made? Better, fairer, bodies than hers could be had for a few rupees!

No, she would try to give him some comfort with her love, her tenderness, the warmth of her body. In a few hours, she would try to compensate for all he had missed so far. In her body, at least for a few moments, Vijay Singh would get something that he had been denied.

And in the years to come, when the rigours of jail life would threaten to make him lose his faith in life, he would be saved by the memory of these few hours. The memory of a girl, of a youthful body. And he would smile. The clouds of frustration would disappear. He would regain his faith in life, his determination to keep alive his body and his mind for the sake of India, for the sake of Revolution.

And one day, when the country would be free, Vijay Singh would come out from prison, not battered and broken in spirit but smiling with hope. Millions would hear the story of his life and his record of sacrifice would make them lift their heads with pride. By then he would have forgotten even the name—Bina.

In the task of revolution, where would be the time to remember an obscure girl? But then, Bina would experience that feeling of triumph that an artist feels when he sees his masterpiece.

Bina got up, opened the door and went into the next room.

THE LAST INTERVIEW

(Bombay, 1987)

In his last interview before his death, Khwaja Ahmad Abbas talks about his last film, *Ek Aadmi*. He had reason to feel triumphant with the release of this film as he overrode Doordarshan's indifference to the film and submitted it to the National Film Development Corporation (NFDC), who took but a moment to give their go-ahead. Suresh Kohli talks to the writer-director.

SK: Since all your films have been commercial failures, what motivates you to make them?

KA: My motivation remains the same. To communicate my thoughts to as large a public as possible. This time I have taken a character and built around him people who come in contact with him and try to influence his life. He is a professor of Sanskrit and he's known as a man with an ideal character. During the last moments of his life, he recalls his youth and finds that he has made many compromises. He's been a victim of many temptations: money, women. In his own final judgment, therefore, he is not as ideal as his students think.

His confidant is his young grandson to whom he reveals the true facts of his life, extracting an oath from him that he will not follow in his footsteps. Many of the frailties clung to him, because of his basic weakness of obeying his father in accepting a woman who was not his choice of a wife, and in the process, victimising his beloved who belonged to a lower caste. This leads to his only son falling in bad company and becoming a criminal. But moments before his death, he forgives his wayward son. For, he realises that it was his weakness which led to the aberration of his son also.

SK: Since you have been describing *Ek Aadmi* as your last cinematic endeavour, is it partially autobiographical?
KA: No, thanks! The only possible comparison could be my age and that of my protagonist (Though I am a few years younger than Anupam Kher is in the film). I did not learn Sanskrit, much less become a specialist in the language, I did not teach at the Simla Institute.

SK: One was talking in terms of similarities of experience. Some of your own acts of omission, moments lived through, finding an outlet in the film.
KA: Well, yes, and no. I don't think I would let anyone know my weak moments in life. Moments that I am, perhaps, trying to relive in the film, I am not strong enough to make public my own guilt.

SK: What in your opinion makes *Ek Aadmi* your most controversial film after *Shehar Aur Sapna* and what is common between the two films?
KA: I don't think *Ek Aadmi* will be controversial unless some critic is bent on taking a controversial line. It is a

simple story though the technique of narration is somewhat odd because it is full of flashbacks which do not follow any familiar line. If anything, it follows the "stream of consciousness" of a dying man. I have not tasted death but this is how I feel that a dying man's consciousness would lead him from one incident to the other. There is nothing in common between *Shehar Aur Sapna* and *Ek Aadmi*, thematically. Except the fact that the former was denied a loan by NFDC and the latter was given one after Doordarshan rejected the script.

SK: Why, and at what point in time, did you stop making films with stars?
KA: In 1958. When my wife was dying, and there were cases filed by two stars who were afraid that I might keep the money due to them. At that time, my wife asked me if I could do something for her before she died. Not knowing what she would ask for, I agreed. And she said, "Break away from the star system. Seeing what they have made of you, I can't bear to look at them." That was a promise I could not turn my back on.

SK: Why do you think Doordarshan rejected your script and why did the NFDC ignore all the normal, bureaucratic delays and give you clearance and money?
KA: Doordarshan has not even acknowledged my letters, much less give me reasons for rejecting my film. Only once, in my old friend Harish Khanna's office, one of his deputies blurted out: *"Sahib, kuch mazaa nahin aaya."* On a gesture of deprecation, he shut up and did not elaborate when I said, "Please elaborate what you mean

by *mazaa.*" After which Harish Khanna tactfully changed the subject. As for NFDC, they must have liked the script, particularly the new technique of stream of consciousness. Luckily, the committee was composed of eminent and well-known scenarists of certain standing and therefore, they got the *mazaa* from the narrative, whatever *mazaa* might mean in the context of Doordarshan.

SK: The film has quite a bit of outdoor shooting: Simla, Bhopal, Delhi etc. Didn't your failing health pose any problems?

KA: No, and yes. My general health is not failing. Only a part of my body towards the left foot is creating problems. There were no problems in Delhi where I was staying with a nephew who is a distinguished doctor. In Bhopal, I was very well looked after by the wife of a friend. I hold this young couple in tremendous esteem. Benaras was only a day's shooting. But Simla was problematic. I had to walk about a mile in the January cold to my hotel since no transportation is permitted on the Mall. I suffered from acute restlessness. But luckily, I had the necessary pills with me. The cold was really terrible in Kufri where we took the snow shots. My fur-lined Russian overcoat, fur-cap and fur boots which I used in the minus 40 degrees Celsius temperature in Moscow came in handy in the minus 4 degree Celsius temperature in Kufri. That's how I survived the cold to take the closing shots of the film. I did the indoors in Bombay, by resetting my house to get the desired effects.